A CASE OF ABUSE

The photograph made the Pony Clubbers gasp. The dog, a long-haired Irish setter, was nothing but skin and bones. His ribs showed plainly under his thin, matted coat, and his dark eyes looked toward the camera with despair.

"He'd been kept chained in a concrete pen that was never cleaned. His water was soiled and he was hardly given enough food to keep him alive," Doc Tock told the Pony Clubbers. "The owners weren't trying to punish him—they just didn't bother to take care of him."

Carole felt tears come to her eyes. She couldn't believe that anyone would allow a helpless animal to suffer so. She glanced at Stevie, who looked horror-struck. "Unbelievable," Stevie whispered.

THE SADDLE CLUB

HORSESHOE

BONNIE BRYANT

A BANTAM SKYLARK BOOK
NEW YORK • TORONTO • LONDON • SYDNEY • AUCKLAND

RL 5, 009-012

HORSESHOE

A Skylark Book / May 1995

Skylark Books is a registered trademark of Bantam Books,
a division of Bantam Doubleday Dell Publishing Group, Inc.
Registered in U.S. Patent and Trademark Office and elsewhere.

"The Saddle Club" is a registered trademark of Bonnie Bryant Hiller.
The Saddle Club design/logo, which consists of
a riding crop and a riding hat, is a
trademark of Bantam Books.

"USPC" and "Pony Club" are registered trademarks of
the United States Pony Clubs, Inc., at The Kentucky
Horse Park, 4071 Iron Works Pike, Lexington, KY 40511-8462

The artist wishes to give special thanks to the Jamaica Bay Riding Academy
in Brooklyn, New York.

ISBN 0-553-48262-9

Published simultaneously in the United States and Canada

Bantam Books are published by Bantam Books, a division of Bantam
Doubleday Dell Publishing Group, Inc. Its trademark, consisting of the
words "Bantam Books" and the portrayal of a rooster, is Registered in U.S. Patent
and Trademark Office and in other countries. Marca Registrada. Bantam
Books, 1540 Broadway, New York, New York 10036.

PRINTED IN THE UNITED STATES OF AMERICA

OPM   0 9 8 7 6 5 4 3

I would like to express my special
thanks to Kimberly Brubaker Bradley for her
help in the writing of this book.

HORSESHOE

"RIDERS, CIRCLE LEFT!"

Carole Hanson swung her horse, Starlight, into a smooth circle. There were many things to think about just to make a horse turn—Carole moved her left hand back slightly, toward her hip, and let her right hand move the same amount forward, keeping an even contact with Starlight's mouth. She sank her weight more heavily into her outside heel, kept her back straight, moved her left shoulder back, and turned her head to look in the direction she wanted Starlight to go. She pressed her left leg against Starlight's side but supported his other side with her right

1

leg. Steady, steady. She made tiny adjustments with her legs, seat, and hands all throughout the circle.

All that, she thought ruefully, for one simple circle —one one-hundredth of the drill she and the rest of the riders in her Pony Club, Horse Wise, were practicing. Yet Starlight had responded perfectly, curving his neck and back in a gentle arch and turning without fuss or hesitation. Carole felt a flush of pride for him. He was doing so well—she had worked so hard to train him. Surely the drill would be a perfect chance to show—

"Carole!" Max Regnery, the head of Horse Wise and the owner of Pine Hollow Stables, shouted across the ring. Carole looked up, startled. "Nice circle, Carole. But don't forget that this is a team effort, okay? Pay attention!" Max was smiling, so Carole knew he wasn't really mad. She knew, too, that he understood how easy it was for her to get totally wrapped up in her riding. Only this time, Carole realized that Outlaw's tail was swishing just under Starlight's nose!

"Sorry, Jasmine," Carole said to the little girl who was riding Outlaw. She pulled Starlight up to avoid a collision.

"That's okay," Jasmine answered, grinning because she almost never saw Carole Hanson make a riding mistake. Everyone knew that Carole was really good.

2

Jasmine moved Outlaw, her own Welsh pony, back to the rail and away from Starlight. "Should we try it again, Max?" she called.

"Again!" Max confirmed.

This time Carole paid attention to Jasmine and Outlaw as well as to Starlight. Horse Wise was made up of both younger and older riders, and in the drill each older rider was paired with a younger one. Carole was supposed to ride the exact same circle as Jasmine and Outlaw, only she had to keep Starlight exactly half a circle away from Outlaw. This wasn't easy, because Starlight's strides were so much bigger than the pony's. Carole had to ride the circle evenly, and at the same time shorten Starlight's strides to match Outlaw's.

"Keep him moving on as much as you can," she whispered to Jasmine. Jasmine nodded and urged Outlaw forward. Carole was pleased to see how well Jasmine was doing. This drill was complicated, and it wasn't easy for some of the younger girls, who hadn't been riding very long.

Across the ring, Stevie Lake was riding her circles with Jackie. Jackie's main problem in the drill was that she sometimes got so enthusiastic that she forgot what she was doing. Stevie sympathized, because she often had the same trouble herself. At the same time,

3

this drill was serious stuff. Not only was she going to have a chance to show off her new horse, Belle, but all their work was going toward a good cause. They were going to perform next week at the Willow Creek Founders' Day fair, in support of the County Animal Rescue League.

Stevie wiped her bangs off her sweaty face, grinned at Jackie, and moved Belle into the next element of the drill. She never minded how hard she worked when she was doing it for a reason she cared about. Stevie was famous for her wild schemes, but she could succeed at serious things too. She and Jackie made a terrific pair.

"All riders cross through the center!" Max commanded. Lisa Atwood moved her horse, Delilah, into position behind May Grover and her new pony, Macaroni. The riders had formed two lines down the long sides of the arena and were crossing through the middle alternately, making a giant X. The trick with crossing through the center was to keep a perfectly even pace. The horses had to be moving at exactly the same speed; otherwise, they would run into each other in the center of the ring. Once they had the drill down pat, they would set it to music, but now they were just trying to get through it without messing up.

4

Luckily for Lisa, Delilah, a sweet palomino mare, listened to Lisa's every instruction. Lisa usually rode Prancer, a high-strung Thoroughbred, but Prancer was not ready for the precision and patience that a drill like this required. Nor, thought Lisa, was she likely to be ready for the Founders' Day parade that they would ride in before their demonstration. Prancer might think she was parading at the racetrack again. Lisa laughed to herself at the thought of Prancer racing through the streets of Willow Creek.

"Hey! What do you think you're doing, you stupid brat? Can't you make that pony move!" Lisa heard the screech from the center of the ring and knew who it was without turning her head. Only one rider at Pine Hollow would talk to one of the little kids like that. Veronica diAngelo.

Sure enough, Veronica had stopped her purebred Arabian, Garnet, in the middle of the ring and was scowling at Jessica Adler. Apparently Jessica had crossed the ring too slowly and had let two riders cross in front of her instead of one, as she was supposed too. It was an easy mistake to make, particularly for such a little girl riding a small pony. Lisa hardly knew Jessica, but she felt sorry for her. Jessica looked as though she were ready to cry.

"*Veronica,*" Max said in a quiet but angry tone that

told Lisa he was feeling the same way. "You didn't help matters by halting your horse. Let's re-form the lines and try it again."

Veronica sniffed and tossed her sleek black hair over her shoulder. "I haven't got all day," she muttered. "This stupid drill is taking up way too much of my time." Lisa saw Max decide not to hear her. Instead, he went up to Jessica and smiled.

"Chin up," he said. "Old Penny's taking advantage of you. You have to show her who's boss." His hand moved affectionately down the pony's neck as he spoke. Penny had been a lesson pony at Pine Hollow for years. Some days she was inclined to be stubborn, and Lisa, seeing the look on the pony's face, knew that this was one of those days. She felt doubly sorry for Jessica.

"Can't we get started?" Veronica demanded. Lisa looked up, annoyed, just in time to see Veronica cut right in front of Michael Grant, a new boy at Pine Hollow. "I believe I'm supposed to ride just in front of you, aren't I?" Veronica asked him, her voice turned honey sweet.

"Sure," Michael said. He slowed down to give Veronica room, but other than that he hardly seemed to notice her, even when Veronica turned and batted her eyelashes at him. Lisa was amazed. Usually boys liked Veronica—at least until they got to know her.

If Michael Grant hadn't noticed Veronica, Stevie thought from across the ring, then he was certainly the only rider who hadn't. Her tantrum had created waves of displeasure throughout the group, and now most of Horse Wise was giving Jessica sympathetic looks.

"She's mean," Jackie hissed to Stevie. "I wouldn't want her to be my big sister."

"I wouldn't want her to be my garbage collector," Stevie replied. She caught the glances of Carole and Lisa, her two best friends, and the three of them shook their heads. Long ago they had formed a club called The Saddle Club. Members had to be horse crazy and willing to help each other out. The Saddle Club had solved a lot of problems, but there wasn't much they could do to help this situation now. Jessica started to cross the ring again, and Stevie crossed her fingers that she would do it right.

Right away Stevie could see what the problem was. Penny was dragging her feet stubbornly, and Jessica was kicking her forward. When Penny sped up, her stride shortened and became choppier, and she didn't really travel any faster. What Jessica needed to do was lengthen Penny's stride, but that was hard to do and

Jessica probably hadn't been riding long enough to be able to do it.

Jessica began to lose ground. One rider crossed between her and Veronica, and she had to be the next person through the center. She gave Penny a desperate kick, and the mare shot forward, galloping—and ran right into Garnet. Garnet squealed and hunched her back, about to kick Penny. Penny saw the kick coming and dodged sideways fast.

Jessica managed to stay on. She threw her weight back into the saddle and rode Penny out of harm's way. Veronica, not expecting Garnet's reaction, fell forward onto Garnet's neck, her fingers clutching Garnet's mane. She seemed to catch her balance, and then—The Saddle Club was willing to swear later that she did it on purpose—she ever so slowly slid to the ground. Her feet hit first, and she whirled to Max, her face purple with rage.

"Did you see what just happened?" she screamed. Stevie looked up at Carole, who nodded and grinned. They'd all fallen off about a zillion times. It was part of riding. Neither of them believed for a second that Veronica was really concerned about her fall.

But Veronica was not finished. "I didn't come here to risk my life!" she shouted. "I didn't come here to risk my purebred horse's life either! I'm not sure why

8

we're even doing this—all this for a bunch of mangy, nasty animals that nobody wants and that aren't worth anything in the first place!"

Lisa winced. The County Animal Rescue League had sounded important to all of them. Veronica never understood anything.

"You know, Veronica," Max said slowly, "participation in this drill is not mandatory. You don't have to be here."

"Good! I'm leaving!" Veronica dusted some imaginary dirt from the seat of her expensive breeches and led Garnet out of the ring. The rest of Horse Wise gave an audible sigh of relief.

"Well," Max said with a wide grin. "That's that. Let's try it again, everybody, shall we? Remember, if this were easy, it wouldn't be a worthwhile exhibition. Start with the circles.

"And, Carole, Jessica's without a big sister now, so keep an eye on her, okay? I'm counting on you to watch *two* young riders." He grinned, and Carole knew he was referring to her earlier inattention. She smiled back. She'd show Max—plus, she'd be a much better big sister than Veronica ever could be!

"Are you okay?" she asked, riding close to Jessica.

Jessica nodded, but Carole could see that her chin was trembling and her eyes were filled with tears.

9

"Don't worry," Carole said. "It's hard, but you'll get it."

"Why do you think she left?" Jessica asked.

"Who? Veronica? Don't worry about her either—she's always a pain in the neck."

Jessica swallowed hard and nodded again, but Carole didn't think she felt better. Penny, indignant at being kicked by Jessica and kicked at by Garnet, got slower and slower as the practice went on, and Jessica never managed to cross through the center correctly. The rest of the practice went well, however, and Max called them to a halt after an hour's hard work.

"Nice job," he said, smiling at every one of them. "All of you did very well. Think about these movements over the next few days, and Tuesday afternoon we'll try setting it to music, okay?"

"Okay, Max!" May Grover shouted almost too enthusiastically. The riders laughed.

"Okay, May," Max said. "All of you, untack your horses, cool them out, and feed them. We'll meet back at my office in"—he checked his watch—"forty minutes. Horse Wise, dismissed!"

Stevie raised her hand. "Max? I've got an idea. Since I think we're still going to need a lot of luck to do well in the drill, I think we should all touch the good-luck horseshoe on our way *into* the barn."

10

Everyone laughed again. The good-luck horseshoe was the best known of the Pine Hollow traditions. The horseshoe hung near the main entrance of the stable. Everyone touched it before they rode, and no one had ever been seriously injured at Pine Hollow. However, no one ever touched it *after* they rode.

"I don't think we need luck to take off a saddle," Lisa said.

"I don't think we'll get hurt filling up the horses' water buckets," Carole added, laughing, and the little riders all giggled.

"Luck," Stevie insisted. "We'll need it for the drill."

"Skill," Max countered. "Not luck. Precision, accuracy, control, careful thinking—"

Stevie shook her head, her face serious. Dismounting Belle, she walked up to the good-luck shoe and gave it a loud slap, like a high-five, as she led Belle into the barn. One by one, all the other riders followed her example.

2

"HOW'RE YOU DOING with Outlaw, Jasmine?" Carole leaned over the door into the stall where her "little sister" was carefully untacking the pony. Carole had just finished taking care of Starlight.

"Pretty well," said Jasmine. She unbuckled the girth and reached up to lift the saddle off Outlaw's back. The saddle was heavy and awkward for her, and she staggered a little. "Except—"

Carole hurried to help her. Where Jasmine reached up for the saddle, Carole reached down, because she was so much taller than Jasmine. She helped Jasmine balance the saddle across her arm.

12

"Thanks," Jasmine said, grinning. "I'll take this to the trailer and be right back to groom him."

"I'll help you," Carole said.

"I don't really need help," Jasmine said, turning to face Carole and walking backward down the aisle. "Really. I'm okay."

Carole waited with Outlaw anyway until Jasmine came back. She offered to help brush him, but Jasmine shook her head. "See, Carole," she said, a serious expression on her face, "when my parents said they would buy me a pony, I promised them that I would take care of it myself. I know they wouldn't mind you helping me, but I'd rather do everything that I can by myself. Besides, I really *like* taking care of Outlaw." She smiled a little anxiously, as if afraid Carole would be offended.

Carole understood right away. "I feel like that myself," she said. "There's nothing I like better than taking care of Starlight. I'll go see how Jessica's doing. You yell if you need me."

Jasmine grinned and nodded, her anxiety gone. Carole went down the aisle to Penny's stall, but before she got there, she could hear muffled thumps and what sounded like a small girl crying. She ran the last few steps and threw open the door.

Penny was whirling in her stall, her head and hindquarters crashing into the walls. Jessica was chasing her, lunging at her head and crying softly, "Stop it! Stop it! *Penny!*"

Carole caught Jessica in her arms before the frantic pony could hurt her. "Hey, hey! Whoa! Jessica, what's wrong?"

Jessica sagged against Carole, covering her face with her hands. "Penny won't come, she hates me!" she wailed. "I can't unbuckle the girth, she won't let me near her, I tried talking nice to her! She hates me!"

Carole knelt in the sawdust and used the edge of her T-shirt to wipe Jessica's face. Penny, standing warily against the back wall of the stall, came forward and began to eat hay. Carole saw what the problem was—Penny was wearing her saddle but not her bridle.

"Penny doesn't hate you," she said, comforting Jessica. "She just got a little wound up today, and she's not behaving. Here." She walked very slowly and cautiously toward the pony's head. Penny eyed her and began to back up, but relaxed when Carole spoke soothingly to her. At last Carole was able to grab a handful of her mane. "Hand me her halter," she said to Jessica.

Jessica ran to get it from its hook on the stall door.

14

She handed it to Carole without saying a word. "Now the lead rope," she said. Jessica gave it to her. Carole tied the other end of rope to a ring built into the stall wall for just that purpose. Penny stood quietly.

"Now," said Carole, "next time, take her saddle off first. That way you can still hold on to the bridle if she starts to move away from you. Or put the halter on first and tie her in the corner. Then she'll stay put when you groom her too.

"And don't ever chase a pony around in its stall like that," she added. "Penny started out thinking it was fun, but she might have decided you were scary and tried to kick you. You could have been hurt. Next time you have trouble, come get me, or Max or Red, or one of my friends. We'll help you."

Jessica nodded and sucked in her breath with a quivering noise that still sounded very much like a sob. "Okay?" Carole asked.

"I guess so." She didn't sound convinced.

Carole felt sorry for her. "Jess, it wasn't your fault," she said. "Penny's being uncooperative and you just don't know all this stuff yet. You'll learn. I didn't know it either when I was your age."

Jessica shrugged. "She hates me," she repeated, and went to get Penny's grooming gear.

Carole wished she knew of something to say to

15

make Jessica feel better. Unfortunately, just as she'd understood how Jasmine felt, she also understood how Jessica felt. Carole could still remember when she didn't know how to control a horse, and she knew that when the horses she rode misbehaved, she had sometimes felt that they had done it on purpose, because they hated her. Now that she was older, she knew that horses had good days and bad days, just like people, but she realized she probably couldn't explain this to Jessica. Instead, she decided to talk about something else, to get Jessica's mind off the pony.

"Did you just move to Willow Creek?" she asked when Jessica came back. She knew Jessica had been riding at Pine Hollow for only a few weeks.

"We moved here six months ago," Jessica answered. "I took riding lessons for about a year where we used to live. My parents work, and for a while they didn't have time to find me another stable." She brushed Penny's ears carefully and smoothed her copper mane.

"We used to move around a lot when I was little too," Carole said. "My dad's in the Marines." Only, Carole thought, her parents made sure they found her a place to ride right away, because they knew how important it was to her. Of course, Marine Corps bases often had riding stables, but still—

16

"Do you have brothers and sisters?" she asked Jessica.

"No."

"Me neither," Carole said.

Jessica continued as if Carole hadn't spoken. "We have a yellow house with eleven rooms and 2.2 acres of land. There are three houses down the road and there are no kids living in any of them." She was brushing Penny's legs now. Carole rested her arms on Penny's back and leaned over to look at her. Jessica's bent head looked sad.

"Who do you play with?" she asked.

Jessica shrugged again. "Just me. I play by myself. The school bus stops at the end of the lane and I walk home from there. I have a snack usually. Sometimes I read, or watch TV. I wait for my dad—he gets home first.

"I know lots of girls at school, but I'm not allowed to go home with them," she continued, "because somebody would have to go pick me up, and my parents don't have time. I can't have anybody over at my house either, because my parents trust me home by myself but they don't trust me home alone with friends. Now I get to come here once a week to ride. I take a different bus." She stood up as she was saying

17

the last part, and Carole was amazed at the soft smile that spread over her face. Clearly, riding was important to Jessica.

"You love horses?" she asked the little girl.

"I love all animals. I love horses best." Jessica took the grooming bucket away from Carole. They untied Penny and shut her stall door, and Jessica went to put the grooming bucket away.

"Thank you—thank you for helping me," she called back to Carole. "I hope I didn't bother you too much."

As soon as Lisa had finished making Delilah comfortable, she went to check on May. As she expected, May was cheerfully grooming Macaroni. Lisa admired the pony which May had just gotten. She had outgrown her old, smaller pony, Luna.

"I like Macaroni an awful lot," May confided. "I loved Luna, but do you know what?"

"What?" asked Lisa.

"Last Saturday I went to visit Luna in her new home. I met the little girl who owns her now, and do you know what?"

"What?" Lisa smiled.

"She loves Luna already almost as much as I do. So I know Luna will be okay. Hey, Lisa, I'm almost done.

Why don't you go help Michael? He keeps asking me where to put things."

Lisa willingly went looking for the new boy, Michael Grant. She found him in the tack room, holding his horse's bridle and looking confused. "Can I help?" she asked him.

"Yeah." Michael held up the bridle and smiled. "I can't remember where this goes. I know it was *one* of these hooks—" He gestured toward the forty or so bridle hooks that lined the walls.

Lisa showed him the correct place, then helped him put his saddle and grooming bucket away. She was just thinking what a nice person Michael seemed to be, and how nice it was to have one boy at Pine Hollow who wasn't infatuated with Veronica diAngelo, when he said, "Can I ask you one more question?"

"Sure," said Lisa.

"Who was that good-looking girl with the black hair in our class? Veronica Somebody—what's her last name?"

Lisa shook her head in disbelief. It was inevitable. "I didn't realize you noticed her," she said.

"It was hard not to notice her!"

"Right," agreed Lisa, "she's the one who was rude about CARL and fell off her horse."

19

"I think she's wrong about CARL," Michael said. "I think we're performing for a good cause. But no, I meant it would be hard not to notice such an attractive girl. And she was certainly well dressed—I mean, her breeches weren't the cheap kind, if you know what I mean, and her boots looked like they were custom-made. And the way her shirt and earrings coordinated and everything—I really admire a girl with a snappy wardrobe."

Lisa looked down at her own clothes. Snappy they weren't. She wore boots and breeches to riding class, but the breeches were old and stained with grass and dirt, and the boots hadn't been polished in—well, in longer than they should have been. Plus she was wearing the MANURE MOVERS OF AMERICA T-shirt her dad had given her for Christmas last year, and it had green stains on her shoulder from where Prancer had nuzzled her. Still, how could Michael judge someone by her wardrobe? It was the sort of thing only Veronica would do. Perhaps, Lisa thought, he and Veronica actually deserved each other.

Michael leaned against a tack trunk and smiled at her. He had a nice smile and good teeth, and he had nice brown hair. It was too bad, thought Lisa, that he was beginning to give her the creeps.

"I have a theory," he said grandly, "I think it's just

as easy to love a rich girl as a poor girl. What do you think?"

Lisa smiled but gritted her teeth. "Her name's diAngelo," she said. "Veronica diAngelo."

"DiAngelo," Michael repeated thoughtfully. "Almost aristocratic, wouldn't you say?"

Lisa made herself smile once more before hurrying away. Yuck! She couldn't wait to tell Stevie and Carole about him!

STEVIE FUSSED OVER Belle until the mare's coat was shining. Seeing a piece of hay floating in Belle's water bucket, Stevie fished it out and brought Belle fresh water and scrubbed the bucket out while she was at it. Once Belle was completely cooled from her ride, Stevie gave her a bucket of grain. Then, sure there was nothing more she could do for her horse, Stevie headed toward Max's office for the Horse Wise meeting.

Halfway there, she stopped and spun on her heel. That Veronica! Stevie wouldn't have believed her eyes, except that it had happened so many times before. Garnet stood in her stall, steaming, sweating, and fully tacked. Her water bucket was empty and she hadn't been given any dinner. Her hayrack was empty too.

"You poor horse," Stevie muttered. "You don't deserve her—she doesn't deserve you. One of these days you'll get tangled up in the reins, the way she just dumps you in your stall."

While she talked, Stevie had been rapidly untacking the mare. Garnet sighed in relief when Stevie undid the tight girth, and nosed Stevie's arm while Stevie unbuckled the bridle.

"You sweet mare," Stevie said. She gave Garnet a vigorous if quick grooming, and refilled her water and hay. Lastly, she gave Garnet the same amount of grain she had just given Belle.

Garnet drank some water and slobbered on Stevie, as if in appreciation. "I get so mad at her when she does this to you," Stevie told her. "Honestly, I wish I knew a way to pay her back."

A FEW MINUTES later, the last members of Horse Wise were crowding into Max's office. Standing at the front with Max was a tall, dark-haired woman they'd never seen before. Max smiled as Stevie, the last rider inside, shut the door and squeezed herself onto a space on the floor in between Carole and Lisa.

"I had to take care of her horse for her!" Stevie hissed indignantly. Her friends nodded sympathetically. They knew without asking who Stevie meant.

"Come to order," Max said, and the riders quieted. "Today I thought we should see firsthand why we're performing this drill. We've all worked hard for the past few weeks, and now here's our chance to see what it's really about. It's my pleasure to introduce to you Dr. Takamura, from the County Animal Rescue League."

The woman smiled and stepped forward. "Most people just call me Doc Tock," she said, smiling at her own funny nickname. "It's really a pleasure for me to come here today. I always enjoy getting a chance to tell people about the work we do at CARL, but I enjoy it even more when I'm talking to a group of young people who love animals as much as I know all of you do.

"I'm a veterinarian—a small-animal veterinarian. That means that I limit my practice to animals like dogs, cats, rabbits, and guinea pigs. Because of CARL, I also work with quite a lot of small wildlife, such as raccoons, squirrels, and foxes. I do some work with birds, but I'm not qualified to take care of protected species like eagles or falcons. We have another vet who does that at CARL. I also don't do exotics like zoo animals, nor do I treat large animals like horses or cows."

May Grover raised her hand. "Do you know Judy Barker? She's our vet." Judy took care of all the Pine Hollow horses.

Doc Tock laughed. "Yes, Judy is a friend of mine. Like me, she has her own practice, but volunteers

24

once a week at CARL. Judy's our equine expert. We always call her whenever we get a horse in—which isn't often. Let me tell you about the sort of animals we usually see. Could somebody please turn off the lights?"

Lisa jumped up to hit the switch, and Max pulled down the window shades. Doc Tock turned on a slide projector. The first picture was one of a small redbrick building. "This is the home of the County Animal Rescue League—better known as CARL. We're fortunate to have our own site, with two acres of outdoor cages, dog runs, and a small paddock. Inside the building"—she switched to a slide of a young woman holding a cat outside a row of cages—"we have a reception room, several treatment and holding rooms, and a full small-animal surgery. The whole facility was funded by donations over several years, and we continue to rely entirely on donations of time, goods, and money.

"Many people volunteer at CARL," she said, smiling at the group. "Many companies give us medicine and vaccines at cost or free, and a local grocery store chain keeps us supplied with dog and cat food. But we still need cash donations to maintain and run the facility.

"That, of course, is not the important thing about CARL. The important thing is the animals we help.

25

Let me introduce you to a few friends of mine." She clicked the slide projector again, and a picture of a yellow dog with a bright, happy face appeared on the screen.

"Ohh!" said several members of Horse Wise.

"This is Champ. He's our mascot," explained Doc Tock. "Champ has been living at CARL for six years, ever since he was badly injured in a car accident and left on the roadside to die. One of our volunteers found him and brought him in. He's perfectly healthy now, and we could easily find him an adoptive family, but his recuperation took so long that we all fell in love with him and none of us wanted to give him up. He's the only permanent resident at CARL. He's a real sweetheart.

"We do sometimes get called to take care of a domestic animal who's been injured, like Champ, but more often our dogs and cats are actually brought in by their owners. Sometimes people overestimate the amount of attention and care a pet needs. Or they buy a cute puppy, but they aren't prepared when it grows up to be a hundred-pound dog."

Doc Tock showed a slide of a mother cat surrounded by kittens. "This cat is a perfect example," she said. "She's a very nice cat, but the owners never had her neutered, and they let her out to roam every

26

night. She'd had kittens five times, they told us, and this time they brought her in to CARL to give birth because they were so tired of her having kittens. It never occurred to them to do something about it before she became pregnant!

"The cat had six very cute kittens. We managed to find good homes for them all, but it wasn't easy—there are too many kittens born around here and not enough people that want to keep them. The cat's owners then came and wanted her back, but we made them agree to neuter her and we performed the surgery before we gave her back to them."

Meg Durham raised her hand. "Doesn't neutering hurt the cat?" she asked.

Doc Tock shook her head emphatically. "No. The animal doesn't understand what it's missing, and the surgery is routine and very safe. Look at it this way. Thousands of unwanted cats and dogs are put to sleep every year. By neutering your pet, you are actually saving lives. Does that make sense?" The members of Horse Wise nodded.

"Good. Neutering and vaccinating pets are both very important, and we try hard to educate the public about these procedures. That's one of our many goals. But CARL is the County Animal *Rescue* League. A lot of what we do involves actually rescuing animals from dangerous or abusive situations. Some people"—her voice tightened—"some horrible people should never be allowed near animals. Here's a dog that was brought in six months ago. He was removed from his home when a neighbor called the sheriff about him. We get a lot of cases that way."

The photograph made the Pony Clubbers gasp. The dog, a long-haired Irish setter, was nothing but skin and bones. His ribs showed plainly under his thin, matted coat, and his dark eyes looked toward the camera with despair.

"He'd been kept chained in a concrete pen that was never cleaned. His water was soiled and he was hardly given enough food to keep him alive. You can't see by the picture, but his feet and haunches were covered with open sores from lying in filth for so long. The owners weren't trying to punish him—they just didn't bother to take care of him."

Carole felt tears come to her eyes. She couldn't believe that anyone would allow a helpless animal to suffer so. She glanced at Stevie, who looked horror-struck. "Unbelievable," Stevie whispered.

"We can't save every animal that we find," Doc Tock said. "Unfortunately, some die despite our best efforts, and others reach us in such bad shape that the only merciful thing to do is put them out of their misery. But this dog had a happy ending."

She switched to the next slide. The same dog, his coat grown full and luxurious, romped on a grassy lawn with two small boys. His tail was a wagging blur and his eyes were bright with joy—as were the eyes of the two little boys.

"After two months in our care he was released to a wonderful family," explained Doc Tock. "At the time he was still timid and rather withdrawn, but after another two months the family sent us this picture. This dog is an example of the sort of thing we do best: rescue an animal from a harmful situation and give him a chance to live out his life the way he should."

Lisa felt a great lump in her throat. She had never seen an abused animal before—looking at the "before" and "after" pictures of the Irish setter made her realize for the first time that the work CARL was doing absolutely needed to be done.

"We also take care of injured wild animals," Doc Tock continued. "Here, for example, is a picture of a turtle who was hit by a car. The family that hit it didn't mean to hit it, and they brought it in to us right away. Fortunately, we were able to heal him and release him back into the wild.

"And this slide shows a family of baby birds. These

infants—robins, although you can't tell in the photograph—were left helpless when their mother was killed by a cat. We were able to raise them and later release them outside our facility. We still see them flying around occasionally."

Doc Tock showed them several more slides of different animals brought in to CARL. She explained in detail the care each received. "That's all I have to show you," she concluded. "I hope this gives you a little taste of what we do at CARL. Thank you for your attention, and remember, all of you are welcome to come visit us at any time. We're open every day until seven P.M. We've always got a vet on call for after-hours emergencies.

"I'm headed off to CARL now. We've got an injured skunk that I think is just about ready to have babies. But first, do you have any questions?"

Polly Giacomin shot up her hand. "What else can we do to help you?" she asked. Several people nodded their heads in agreement. After seeing the slides, all of the Pony Clubbers wanted to help.

"I think what you're doing now is pretty wonderful," Doc Tock said. "Your drill will raise awareness about CARL as well as raise money for us. Beyond that, make sure you treat your own animals with love and care. Neuter and vaccinate your pets, and if you know of an injured or helpless animal, be sure to give us a call."

Doc Tock held up a warning finger. "That's important, so I ought to stress it. Be sure to give *us* a call. Don't attempt to rescue the animal yourselves. Injured animals often lash out at people, and you could be hurt by them or hurt them worse by trying to restrain them. We're trained to do it, so leave the rescuing to us. Okay?"

"Okay," everyone said.

"You've really been a super group," she said. "Thank you very much!" As she left the room, Horse Wise applauded her vigorously.

"Well," said Max, "I don't think anything I can say right now could top Doc Tock's excellent presentation. I do still need to discuss the logistics of next weekend with all of you. But it's well past noon, and I'm starving. Let's break for lunch and meet back here in one hour. Horse Wise, dismissed!"

Lisa sat still while everyone else jumped to their feet. She had hardly heard Max—she was so deeply touched by Doc Tock's presentation. "After all the good they're doing," she muttered, "all that we're doing for them is marching some horses around?" Suddenly, despite what Doc Tock had said, she didn't feel that it was nearly enough.

31

"Come on." Carole grabbed her by the arm and hauled her to her feet. "Whatever you're thinking about, it can wait until we get to the back pasture."

"Back pasture?" Lisa, thinking only about CARL, was confused.

"Time for lunch," said Carole.

"Time," said Stevie, "for a Saddle Club meeting."

THE THREE GIRLS took their sack lunches to a grassy hillside overlooking the ring where they had just practiced their drill. It was one of their favorite places to sit and talk at Pine Hollow.

"Okay, Lisa," Stevie began, unwrapping her peanut butter and jelly sandwich, "tell us what's bugging you. Why didn't you hear Max say it was time for lunch?"

Lisa sighed. She didn't know quite how to begin. "It's not that I'm not glad we're doing the drill," she said. "I am. I think it will be a nice drill, but it seems like—I don't know—such a drop in the bucket. Such a small thing, compared to what CARL really needs. I mean, we're only asking for donations. How much are

33

people going to pay just to watch some Pony Clubbers do a drill?"

"It'll be a very good drill," Carole replied. "Now that we've gotten rid of Veronica—"

"No matter how good, it isn't going to be good enough," Lisa insisted. "I'd like to do something else for CARL—something that would really make a lot of money." She opened her lunch and pulled out a sandwich. "What do you think?"

Carole smiled warmly. "I think it's a good idea," she said. "I'm sure the three of us can think of something." They lay back on the warm grass and watched the clouds chase one another across the sky. Lisa had a thermos of homemade lemonade that she shared with Carole and Stevie.

"Here's an idea," Stevie said, sitting up excitedly. "We could start a horseback messenger service, like the Pony Express, only we could run messages for the businesses in Willow Creek. Carole on Starlight and me on Belle—"

"—and me on Prancer," said Lisa, laughing. "I'd be the fastest messenger of all."

"It would be a lot of fun," Carole said, tugging at Stevie's hair, "but I think everyone has fax machines these days, and no matter how fast we were, I think that they'd be faster. Why don't we have a bake sale?"

34

"Oh, sure," Stevie answered, grinning. "I hate to remind you, Carole, but so far the only thing we've baked successfully has been Rice Krispie treats. I don't think Rice Krispie treats alone qualify as a bake sale." She flopped back on the grass. "Maybe a makeup make-over booth. Like at the mall, where they show you how spectacular you'd look with eye shadow and lip gloss—"

"I hate to remind *you*, Stevie," Carole replied, "but I believe you once turned your own hair green."

"I don't think we could take people's money and then turn their hair green," Lisa said. "But anyway, I'm glad we have some ideas. We'll think of something. I'm glad you guys want to help CARL too."

"You bet," said Stevie. "We're behind you."

"One hundred percent," said Carole. She added, "There's another person I wish we could help, and that's Jessica Adler." Briefly she told them about Jessica's trouble untacking Penny, and how lost and lonely Jessica had seemed. "She's a latchkey kid, and I think it's hard on her," said Carole.

"I was kind of a latchkey kid," Stevie objected. "Both my parents always worked, and it wasn't hard on me."

"I'm sort of a latchkey kid now, and so is Carole," said Lisa. "But we're a lot older than Jessica. Think

35

about what you did when you were her age, Stevie. Who took care of you?"

Stevie frowned, considering. "Michael was still pretty little, and anyway, with me and Alex and Chad always playing tricks on each other, my parents would never have left us alone. They used to hire college students to watch us every day after school, and then they'd hire another student to take care of us during the summer. We did all the normal stuff—went swimming, played with the neighbors. My brothers were all in Little League, and I rode. I could always walk to Pine Hollow if I wanted to." She took a long sip of lemonade. "It's not that I didn't notice that my parents weren't there, but they made sure we were well taken care of. We always had plenty of stuff to do."

"That's the problem with Jessica, I think," explained Carole. "She doesn't have neighborhood kids to play with, and she doesn't have anything else to do. She comes here once a week to ride, plus she's joined Horse Wise. That's all she has. I think we should try to be nice to her, and help her make some friends."

They all agreed. "Poor kid," Carole continued, "she seemed so upset about Veronica too."

"Speaking of Veronica," Lisa cut in, "you know how Michael Grant seemed entirely oblivious of her presence in class?"

36

"Uh-huh," said Stevie. "I took it as a sign of true intelligence. It's about time we got some decent boys around here."

"Not so fast," said Lisa. "I'm afraid he wasn't as oblivious as he seemed." She described her conversation in the tack room. When she mimicked Michael, saying, "It's just as easy to love a rich girl as a poor girl," The Saddle Club hooted with laughter.

"That's rich," gasped Carole. "I'm out of the running, then. I spent most of this month's allowance on polo wraps for Starlight."

"And I," said Stevie, "don't have any snap left in my wardrobe!" She waved her ragged shirttail at her friends, and they all howled again. Stevie liked to wear old jeans and battered cowboy boots when she rode, and no one had ever seen her in designer clothes.

"I decided that Michael and Veronica might actually deserve each other," Lisa said.

"Well, I hope Veronica doesn't get him," Stevie said, suddenly fierce. "She's so lazy and stuck-up that she shouldn't ever get anything she deserves—not even a dweeb like Michael Grant. First she was mean to Jessica, then she pulled that stunt, pretending to fall off, then she left Garnet tacked up in her stall! She didn't even loosen the girth!"

37

Carole flinched. Veronica's first horse, Cobalt, whom Carole had loved, had died because Veronica had jumped him carelessly. "She'll cause another accident," Carole said.

"I wish she'd *have* an accident, like in front of a speeding truck," Stevie said. "She makes me so mad. I'd like to teach her a lesson." The others nodded in agreement.

They spent another pleasant half hour basking in the sunshine and watching some of the horses turned out in the paddock nearby. Carole had brought some of her father's chocolate chip cookies, and Stevie split her orange three ways. When they saw May Grover come out of the stable and wave her arm at them, they knew it was time for the Horse Wise meeting to resume.

Max started by going through a list of all of the equipment they would need to bring with them for the drill next weekend. "Red will bring the horses in the van," he said. "And I think it would be best to ship them with their saddles on, to save confusion at the start of the parade. Fly sheets on over the saddles, halter, and lead ropes—we'll bridle them after they're unloaded, okay?"

Carole, to Stevie's and Lisa's amusement, was taking notes. She could be very organized where horses were concerned.

"I don't know what the facilities for water will be," Max continued. "So, to be on the safe side, we'll want all our five-gallon jugs filled and in the van. This means water buckets too, and I think you riders should bring something to drink for yourselves as well. You might get pretty thirsty after the parade. We'll have several hours between the parade and the drill, so you'll have plenty of time to walk around the fairgrounds and enjoy the rest of Founders' Day."

Lisa noticed a ripple of excitement pass through the younger riders. It's all starting to feel real to them, she thought. Before this it was just hard work, but now they're beginning to think it will be fun. She saw May nudge Jackie and giggle. Jackie giggled too, and without thinking nudged the rider next to her, who happened to be Jessica Adler. Jessica giggled and nudged Jasmine, who was sitting next to her.

Lisa nudged Carole and pointed toward the giggling, squirming girls. Carole smiled. It was the first time she'd seen Jessica look entirely happy. "That's better," she whispered to Lisa. "That's what she needs, to feel like she belongs."

"We'll help her," Lisa said. "We'll think of something."

"Let's discuss this parade," Max said, turning a stern face toward May and her friends. "I don't want any of you giggling there!" He shook his finger at them solemnly, and it set them off giggling again. Max relaxed his stance and smiled. "Seriously," he said. "I want you all to conduct yourselves as though you were at a horse show or a Pony Club rally. You don't have to look like you're riding in a funeral procession, but I don't want you goofing off either. Also remember that the crowd or unexpected noises—a fire engine, a balloon popping—might make some of the horses nervous. Be prepared. Ride well, don't act like tourists. Okay?"

"Okay, Max," they chorused. Even the little girls were paying attention now.

"Remember that asphalt is slippery," he continued. "Don't ride any faster than a walk. We'll form a sort of procession at the start, and I want you to maintain it as best you can. I want you looking *good*—your best show turnout, Pony Club pins in your helmets, hair neatly braided or up in a *net,* Stevie Lake—"

Stevie raised her eyebrows in mock surprise.

"—and, incidentally, heels down, backs straight, hands quiet. That goes double, of course, for the drill."

Max then passed out a timetable for the following

Saturday and went over it in detail. "That's all," he said at last. "Thank you for your attention during this long meeting. Don't forget our special meeting on Tuesday to finish up the drill. Horse Wise, dismissed!"

As the room emptied, Lisa noticed a pile of brochures sitting on Max's desk. They were about CARL; Lisa remembered Doc Tock saying she would leave some behind. Thoughtfully Lisa picked one up. She put it in her backpack to read later.

JUST AS SCHOOL ended on Monday, the assistant princi-
pal found Lisa to tell her that her mother had called.
Lisa, fearing trouble, hurried to the phone.

"Oh, no, dear," her mother said calmly. "It's just
that poor Miss Adams has the flu, and she's canceled
your ballet class this afternoon. And the store just
called to ask if I could come in and work for someone
else who has the flu. I'm leaving now, so I won't be
home when you get there. I wanted to let you know."

"That's fine, Mom. Thanks." Lisa hung up the
phone pleased to have an unexpected free afternoon.
She didn't mind ballet because she thought it would
improve her balance for riding, but she didn't love it

either, and she certainly didn't mind missing class. She walked down the hallway to look for Carole, but Carole had already left on the bus that would take her to Pine Hollow. Carole went to see Starlight nearly every day.

And Stevie, Lisa thought with a sigh as she started to walk home, had an orthodontist appointment right after school. She wouldn't be able to do anything either. Still, Lisa felt like she ought to spend the afternoon doing something special. It was a beautiful day, bright and clear, and she shouldn't waste it by staying inside. With a flash of inspiration she dug into her backpack and pulled out the brochure Doc Tock had left behind. Where exactly was CARL?

The address and a map were printed on the back page. It was a little far for walking—two miles—but she could easily ride her bike there. Doc Tock had said that they could visit anytime.

Lisa hurried home. She dropped her books in her bedroom, ran a comb through her ponytail, and scribbled a note for her parents, *Back for dinner*. Then she went out to the garage and dusted off her bike. She didn't ride it much anymore, now that she rode horses.

The trip to CARL, along winding back roads, was quick and peaceful. A small wooden sign marked the driveway, and the building looked just as it had in Doc Tock's slide. Lisa parked her bike and walked in the main door.

A receptionist looked up at her and smiled. Before Lisa could speak, a big brown and yellow dog came around the desk to meet her. "Champ!" said Lisa. She bent to pet him, and his tail beat furiously against the floor.

"Have you been here before?" the receptionist asked.

"No," said Lisa, "but I heard all about Champ. I'm Lisa Atwood. I'm a member of Horse Wise Pony Club, and Doc Tock came to talk to us. She said we could visit anytime."

"I'm Letty," the receptionist said, "and Dr. Takamura is the vet working here today. Wait just a sec and I'll get her for you."

When Doc Tock came in, Lisa began to introduce herself again, but Doc Tock held up a hand. "You're with the Pony Club, right?" she asked.

"Yes. I'm Lisa Atwood," Lisa said again.

"I remember your face," Doc Tock said. "Would you like to see the place?" Lisa nodded. "I'll be happy to show it to you, but let me finish up this one job first. Come on in." She stepped into one of the treatment rooms, and Lisa followed.

44

Inside, on a stainless-steel examining table, was a large cardboard box. Inside the box, nestled on a white towel, were three baby raccoons. Lisa exclaimed with delight.

"I'm vaccinating them for rabies," said Doc Tock. "Put on a pair of these gloves and you can hold them for me."

The raccoons were the cutest babies Lisa had ever seen—all bright eyes, long noses, and long-fingered paws. They sniffed Lisa's fingers busily while she held them, and one of them tried to catch hold of her hair. "They're so adorable," said Lisa. "I'd love to have one for a pet. Are they up for adoption?"

"No," said Doc Tock, capping the last of the syringes and throwing it away. "No, Lisa. These are wild animals, and we never put wild animals up for adoption. They aren't meant to be pets. They're cute and easy to care for now, but they grow up to be big raccoons with wild raccoon instincts. They're much happier in the wild—what we want to do is be sure they are healthier in the wild too." She picked up the box and carried it out of the room, motioning for Lisa to follow.

The next room was long and bright and filled with many different types of animal cages. Doc Tock settled the baby raccoons back into their own cage, and they immediately began to romp and play.

"On this side," Doc Tock explained, "we keep cages just for animals that come in for neutering. We run a low-cost spay and neuter clinic, and we've always got some clients." Lisa peered into some of the cages. A dog, evidently recently back from surgery, blinked sleepily at her, and a cat arched its back against the cage door.

Farther down the room Lisa met some of the animals who were recovering from accidents that had brought them to CARL. In one pen she saw the baby skunks that Doc Tock had predicted would be born on Saturday. "Were they really born on Saturday?" she asked.

"You bet. Just a half hour after I returned here. Not that I really needed to do anything, but since the mother is slightly injured, I thought someone should be around in case there were problems. There weren't, though, and the whole family will be released to the wild just as soon as the mom can make it on her own." Doc Tock checked the mother skunk over briefly as she talked.

"Are they really better off in the wild?" Lisa asked. "I mean, they were hurt in the first place in the wild.

They wouldn't be here otherwise." She still wished she could have one of the baby raccoons.

"Well, no," said Doc Tock, pausing to consider Lisa's question. "No, that's not exactly true. They're usually here because of human interference with their life in the wild—they were hit by cars, wounded by hunters, that sort of thing.

"These really aren't domestic animals, Lisa. In most cases they can't be trained, the way horses can, and in some cases they can't even be tamed." She smiled and patted Lisa's shoulder. "I can see you really care about them," she said. "Trust me. They're happier with their freedom."

They continued outside to the dog runs. "Domestic animals, on the other hand, sometimes suffer from too much freedom. This friendly dog is a perfect example." Doc Tock opened the first pen and she and Lisa stepped inside. A big yellow dog leapt toward them. It jumped up and down under Lisa's nose, wagging its tail with delight.

"He's wonderful," said Lisa, throwing her arms around him. The dog, overjoyed, licked her clear across her face and smeared muddy paw prints down the front of her shirt. Lisa, laughing, pushed him away. "Maybe too wonderful," she said.

"Exactly," said Doc Tock. She refilled the dog's water bowl and they stepped back outside the pen, but first they had to push the enthusiastic dog away several more times. Doc Tock sighed and gave the dog a final pat through the wire mesh of the fence.

"His name is Trump," she said. "His owner was a busy executive who never took the time to train him. When he was a puppy it didn't matter, but now that he's a grown dog the man says he can't manage him. There isn't an ounce of meanness in him though, and I'm sure we'll be able to find him a good home. Someone will think he's worth the trouble of training."

"Is he a golden retriever?" asked Lisa. "He looks like it."

"No, he's a mixed breed, but he's probably got a lot of retriever in him. If he were purebred I doubt he'd be here—the owner might have thought he was worth the expense of professional training."

"I'm sure someone will love him," Lisa said. She stood watching Trump while Doc Tock checked another dog. For a moment she considered adopting him herself. Then she checked the idea—she already had a dog, a little Lhasa apso named Dolly. Lisa was reasonably sure that Dolly wouldn't like Trump at all. Besides, Lisa wasn't sure that she had time to train

Trump either. He deserved a better owner the second time around.

Doc Tock came back to Lisa. "I know you like horses," she said.

"Like them?" asked Lisa. "I *love* them."

Doc Tock smiled but didn't look at all happy. "Then try not to be too upset with what I'll show you next," she said. "We don't often have horses here, but we do have one now, and he's not good. He was severely abused."

They turned the corner to face a small paddock. At one end, a tiny wooden stable held two stalls. The paddock was bright with good green grass, but the horse stood in the center as if he were unaware of the grass and everything else around him.

Lisa gasped, and tears came to her eyes. She gripped the top rail of the paddock fence so tightly that later she found splinters in her palms, but she couldn't feel anything right then except horror. Someone had done this to a horse.

He was a bay—or would have been a bay, Lisa thought. His coat was dull and rough from bad food and no grooming, and in many places the hair had fallen out entirely, leaving raw patches of open skin. His scraggly tail was hunched between his

49

back legs. His ears hung almost flat and his eyes were dull.

"Look at his feet," Doc Tock said quietly.

Lisa stared. She knew that some horses, particularly those that weren't ridden often, didn't need to wear shoes, but she also knew that all horses needed their feet trimmed regularly. This horse's feet had not been trimmed; they had been allowed to grow out like great curving sled runners and here and there big pieces of hoof wall had chipped away. Lisa winced, knowing how it must hurt him to walk and even to stand.

"His name is Sal," said Doc Tock.

"Sal," Lisa repeated. "Can I go up to him?"

"If you walk quietly. But, Lisa—don't pet him. He's still covered with fleas and ticks. I don't want you to catch any."

Lisa pulled a handful of tall grass and walked slowly up to Sal's side. He stood unblinking, not trying to move away, or, even, thought Lisa, acting like he knew she was there. She held the grass under his nose. He inhaled slowly and moved his ears halfway forward. Slowly, very slowly, he reached out his top lip and took a few blades of grass. Then he sighed and dropped his head again.

Lisa looked at him closely. His bones showed

clearly beneath his skin. Along one side were some ragged scars—spur marks, or a whip? One hind leg hung slack, and Lisa could see that it was not because he was merely resting, but because he had a festering sore just above his hock.

"He hardly even ate the grass, and he isn't grazing," Lisa said as she slipped back through the fence near Doc Tock.

"I'm surprised that he paid as much attention to you as he did," she replied. "Lisa, this poor horse is one of the worst cases I've seen in years. What you see is only part of the problem—he's got raging parasite infestations. He's so malnourished that I'm not sure he's strong enough to withstand the treatment he has to have. Old Sal might not make it."

"How could someone do this to a horse?" Lisa cried.

Doc Tock put a comforting hand on her arm. "The owner is being brought up on criminal charges," she said with a voice of grim satisfaction. "He left this horse in a tiny pen with not enough grass to survive and only the rainwater that pooled in one corner to drink. He left town for a few months, and forgot him. I don't know how people do it, Lisa, but once in a while they do."

Lisa swallowed hard. "I just can't believe he's going

to die," she whispered. "He seems like such a nice animal." Tears trickled slowly down her cheeks.

"He is. He's been willing and cooperative about everything we've done. That might not be enough." She steered Lisa away from the paddock. "Come inside and let's have something to drink. I can see you're upset. Lisa, you shouldn't be."

Over a glass of cold fruit juice Doc Tock tried to reassure Lisa some more. "After all, our job here at CARL is the good side. We're doing good work. We're saving many animals. Lisa, this is a place of joy—even if we don't accomplish everything we want to.

"Think of it this way. This little horse, Sal, might die here. But if he does, at least his last days will be spent in comfort, with kind people caring for him. The love he gets here may be the first love he's ever received."

Lisa agreed. That much at least made sense to her. "If he lives, maybe I can help you find him a good home," she offered. "Max Regnery, our instructor at Pine Hollow, knows a lot of people who work with horses."

"That'd be great," Doc Tock said. "We'd like your help. I'll let you know how Sal does."

Riding home, Lisa thought she could hardly bear to hear it if Sal died. She wanted him to live—she wanted to see him grow healthy and strong, and play in his paddock and graze like the horses at Pine Hollow. But she understood all Doc Tock had said, and she was more convinced than ever that CARL needed support. The Saddle Club would have to think of something.

6

When Lisa got home, she had only one thought on her mind. They had to have a Saddle Club meeting. Now. She called Stevie.

"They tightenedth all the wireth on my teeth," Stevie said. "I can'th talk."

"We need to have a meeting," Lisa insisted. "Suck on a Popsicle, your mouth will feel better. I'll be over in five minutes and we can walk to Pine Hollow. I know that's where Carole is."

"Where elth would thee be?" agreed Stevie.

At Pine Hollow they found that Carole had just finished Starlight's workout. She greeted them gladly. "We just had the best ride," she said enthusiastically.

"You should have seen him! I set up a jump course in the ring, and he just flew!" She patted Starlight's sweating flank.

"Wonderful!" said Stevie. "Not that he ever isn'th —I mean isn't." Carole looked at her quizzically. "Orthodontith," Stevie explained.

"We came to have a Saddle Club meeting with you," Lisa said. "I've got something I need to tell you two about right away."

"Can it wait until I get Starlight cooled out?"

"Of course!"

Carole walked Starlight for several minutes and then got a bucket of warm water and sponged his sweaty coat. Lisa helped scrape him dry while Stevie put Carole's tack away. Once they had Starlight settled, they headed for the hillside overlooking the ring.

"I just went to CARL," Lisa said. "You wouldn't believe all the stuff I saw."

"Champ?" asked Stevie, who remembered Doc Tock's talk. She grimaced and ran her finger over her braces. "They're not hurting so much now," she admitted. "That Popsicle idea was a good one."

"I saw Champ, but I also saw a lot of animals who were hurting," Lisa said. "Some of them were wild animals, and some were just neglected. There was this perfectly beautiful dog named Trump—his only problem was that no one had taken the time to train him."

"That's terrible," said Carole. "I know how important it is to train animals properly—horses are so strong that they can be really dangerous if they aren't well trained."

"This dog is almost as big as a pony. But that wasn't the bad part," Lisa said, resolutely bringing them back to her story. "They had a horse."

"A horse?" Carole and Stevie leaned forward.

Lisa's eyes filled with tears as she recalled the horse in CARL's paddock. "I can't help it," she said. "He was the saddest thing I ever saw. His name is Sal." She covered her face with her hands.

Stevie and Carole put their arms around her. "CARL will take care of him," Stevie reassured her.

Carole remembered some of the horses she had seen when she went on rounds with Dr. Judy Barker. One had caught tetanus from a filthy stall, and died. Carole thought she knew exactly how Lisa was feeling. "I've seen some awful things too," she said.

"But this poor horse has everything wrong," Lisa said. "Nothing's right with him. And they're doing everything they can to save him, but it might not be enough. Doc Tock said he might die." She described Sal's condition to them—his coat, his sores, his feet.

56

"Worst of all, he just looked so *hopeless*. Like he didn't expect anything good ever to happen to him. Even when I gave him grass, he didn't look happy. He could barely eat it."

Carole sucked in her breath. Stevie pulled up a clump of grass and angrily threw it into the air. "It isn't right," she said.

"That's why we have to think of a good Saddle Club project," Lisa said. "Not just some wild idea to raise money. We need an idea that will really work. It's critical—without our help, animals like Sal don't have a future!"

They sat silently for a moment, thinking hard. "That's it," Lisa said softly.

"What?" asked Carole.

"The future. We can set up a fortune-telling booth on Founders' Day. Everyone wants to know their future!"

"Not if it's bad news," objected Stevie.

"It won't be bad news," Lisa countered. "How could it be? We'll be making the stuff up—we can make it only good news. We can even call the booth Horseshoe. What's better luck than the Pine Hollow horseshoe?" She grinned at her friends.

"I like it," Carole said slowly. "I really like it!"

Stevie nodded. "Me too. You know, Chad's got an

old tent from Boy Scouts that we could use for the booth. We can get some silver stars and whaddyacallems—zodiac signs—and decorate the outside."

"And a giant horseshoe," said Lisa. "And a sign."

"I've got this great purple scarf that looks just like a Gypsy scarf," Carole said. "And I think my mom had some big dangling hoop earrings—like people wore in the seventies. They'd be perfect!"

"And my dad has a paperweight in his office that looks just like a crystal ball," said Stevie. "I'm sure he won't care if we use it—especially if we don't tell him about it until after we're done."

"What else do fortune-tellers do?" asked Carole.

"They read tea leaves. We could get some tea," suggested Lisa. "Not instant, or the stuff in bags—it needs to be loose tea, like I had in England. You get clumps of leaves left over in your cup, and you swirl them around—the swirls are supposed to mean something."

"Like what?" asked Stevie.

"Oh, I don't know," Lisa replied impatiently. "It doesn't matter."

"We could get some books and try to find out. There must be books somewhere that explain this stuff." Carole looked thoughtful.

"Not on your life," replied Stevie. "Between getting

Belle ready for the drill and getting all of this Gypsy stuff together, I'm going to have quite enough to do this week. I certainly won't have time to go to the library."

"Anyway," interjected Lisa before Carole could begin to argue, "if we needed any sort of books, they'd be on acting, not on fortune-telling. Everyone knows that fortune-telling is just for fun. What we need to do is make our fortunes sound believable, so everyone feels satisfied and we draw a big crowd. The important thing is raising money for CARL."

Carole thought about this. "We'll need cards," she said finally.

"You mean tarot cards?" asked Lisa.

Carole grinned. "It doesn't matter," she said, "since none of us can read them anyway."

7

"OHH-HH, MICHAEL! I didn't know I was going to be lucky enough to see you today! Have you joined my riding class?"

There were times, Lisa thought disgustedly, when Veronica diAngelo positively purred. She watched Veronica sidle Garnet up to Michael Grant's side. Across the ring, Stevie took one hand from the reins and made gagging motions. Lisa nodded and made Delilah trot across the ring, away from the revolting pair.

As she passed them she could hear Michael say in a perfectly ordinary tone, "No, I haven't joined your class. This is an extra Horse Wise practice."

"You mean you're doing that stupid drill—I mean, you're practicing your drill exercise?" Veronica asked him, fluttering her eyelashes alluringly.

"Looks like she's got a twitch," Stevie said to Lisa.

"Well!" Everyone could hear Veronica's reply to Michael's murmured assent. "I'm not sure why I wasn't told! After all, this is supposed to be my riding lesson!"

Lisa knew exactly why Veronica hadn't been told— because of her earlier tantrum, she'd left Horse Wise too soon to hear Max announce the extra drill practice. Max, however, was conciliatory.

"I should have called to tell you the schedule changed," he said to Veronica. "Since you're already in the saddle, why don't you just ride around the ring? You know the drill well enough to stay out of everyone's way. Afterward, I'll set up some cavalletti for you and Garnet to work through."

That, thought Lisa, was more than fair. Veronica, however, didn't seem to agree. With her nose held high, she began riding Garnet in circles around the ring—regardless of where the other Pony Clubbers were riding.

"Hey!" shouted May, pulling Macaroni to a halt as Veronica cut directly in front of her. "You're in my way!"

61

"Sorry," Veronica said sarcastically. "Max, this just isn't fair. I don't have room."

"You need to make room for the drill, Veronica, not the other way around." Max sounded measurably less agreeable than he had the first time, Lisa thought.

"Excuse me, Stevie." Veronica next swung Garnet's hindquarters around in front of Belle.

"I wouldn't do that again if I were you," Stevie warned her. She transferred her crop from her outside to her inside hand and gave Veronica a meaningful glare. A crop was a mild type of whip used to get a horse's attention when it misbehaved or wasn't listening. Crops were short, but long enough, Lisa guessed, for Stevie to whack Veronica with hers if she tried. Lisa grinned in admiration. Sometimes she wished she could be as bold as Stevie.

She had her chance a few minutes later, when Veronica cut in front of her. Imitating Stevie, she said not a word in reply to Veronica's insincere apology— she merely held her crop up, and glared. After that Veronica left The Saddle Club alone, but she continued to get in the way of the other riders.

The worst part was that every time someone had to yank their horse to a halt to avoid hitting Veronica, it messed up the precise patterns of the drill. Several times they had to start over, and they hadn't tried to set it to music yet. Lisa could feel the frustration mounting among the members of Horse Wise. If they didn't relax and concentrate, they'd never be able to get it right.

Finally, with only a few minor interruptions, they managed to get to the part where they crossed through the center. Carole, remembering her earlier conversations with Jessica Adler, felt very concerned that Jessica get it right. Jessica needed to feel that she could do it, Carole thought. As soon as she herself had crossed the center and changed directions, she turned in the saddle to watch Jessica cross.

Penny was feeling more cooperative, and Jessica was trying hard. Carole saw her use her legs to urge, not kick, Penny, and at the same time loosen her hold on Penny's mouth. She's learning fast, Carole thought in admiration. She's really getting it. Penny began to respond just as she should, lengthening her strides and covering more ground without really picking up speed —when Veronica cut through the center.

Jessica, panicked, hauled Penny to an abrupt halt. Veronica looked down at her coolly, trotting past with perfect ease. "Haven't you gotten this figured out yet?" she asked the little girl. Jessica, her face white, began to cry. Veronica, Carole saw with utter fury, didn't even notice—she just swept Garnet around the

63

corner of the ring and looked for more riders to annoy.

Carole broke out of the drill pattern and rode Starlight to Jessica's side. "I've had enough of Veronica," she whispered fiercely. "I can't believe what she just did to you. I'm going to ask Max to make her leave right now."

Jessica looked horror-struck. "No!" she cried.

"It's not your fault. She's being ridiculous, and she shouldn't be allowed to upset everyone like this."

"No," Jessica begged. "Please, Carole, I don't want Veronica to leave." She looked even more upset.

"Okay," Carole said unwillingly. "If you really want her to stay, I won't say anything to Max." Not that Max needs me to say something, she thought. He has eyes, and surely he can see what a distraction Veronica is being.

"I really want her to stay," Jessica said. "I do."

"You're doing fine." Carole switched the subject and tried to reassure her. "Don't worry—you were riding just right before Veronica got in your way." She rode Starlight back to the rail, wishing there were more she could do for Jessica.

Carole was correct in thinking that Max had noticed Veronica. She saw him looking straight at the office window, and then give a funny jerk of his head.

64

What was that all about? she wondered. She had her answer a moment later, when Mrs. Reg, Max's mother and Pine Hollow's stable manager, came out of the office looking grim.

"Veronica," she called sharply, "come here."

Veronica tossed her head and rode Garnet to the side of the ring. No one ever disobeyed Mrs. Reg.

"I have something that needs doing in the stable," she said, "and since you're not part of the drill, I want you to do it. Come inside. You can rejoin the lesson when drill practice is over."

Veronica dismounted and sulkily led Garnet inside. The drill team members looked at one another with undisguised relief. Stevie, bending down over Belle's neck, got a good look inside the stable door. Mrs. Reg was handing Veronica a pitchfork and pointing inexorably toward a row of stalls.

"She's going to clean stalls!" Stevie cried with glee. Muffled laughter went around the group—except, Carole noticed, for Jessica, who still seemed too upset to laugh.

"All right, Miss Lake," Max said, but didn't bother to hide his smile. "All of you, let's try it once more from the top. And concentrate!"

With Veronica gone, practice went much more smoothly. After two times through without music,

Max turned on the tape recorder. With music, the drill went even better. Max had selected different music to accompany each section of the drill, and since the music always matched the movement, it made the drill easier to remember. It also, thought Stevie, made it easier to ride smoothly—the music seemed to inspire both the riders and the horses to move in a rhythm, as if they were dancing. I'm dancing with my horse, she thought, and giggled.

Carole was concerned. Though there was no denying that practice went much better without Veronica, she was worried about the effect Veronica had had on Jessica.

Carole was sure that Jessica had been about to correctly lengthen Penny's stride when Veronica got in her way. Now Jessica didn't seem able to do it again—Carole could see her trying, but her rhythm was always off. Either she kicked Penny the way she used to and Penny shortened her stride, or she threw her hands forward too much and Penny cantered, or she didn't give with her hands at all and Penny's trot didn't change.

No matter what, Jessica managed to cross over in the right order, but the differences in pace or gait were noticeable—and would be noticeable, Carole realized, even to people who didn't ride, like the people who would be watching the drill. Carole knew that this was a very small flaw in a complicated drill, but she also knew that Jessica would feel bad if she didn't get it right.

After class Carole hurried to settle Starlight so that she could talk to Jessica. "Can I help you?" she asked, going into Penny's stall. This time, she noticed, Jessica had Penny tied securely in the corner.

"Okay," said Jessica. "If you want to." Carole helped her lift the saddle from Penny's back. "I don't know why you want to," she continued. "If I had a horse as beautiful as Starlight, I'd spend all of my time taking care of *him*."

Carole set the saddle down outside the stall and brought the grooming bucket in. She handed Jessica a brush and they began working on opposite sides of Penny. "You're right, I love taking care of Starlight," she said. "But I didn't come down here to help you take care of Penny. I came down here to see how you were."

"Oh."

"You looked really upset today, and I didn't think you should be," Carole continued. "It was wrong of Veronica to pull out in front of you like that, but you shouldn't take it personally. She's like that toward everyone."

"No," Jessica replied. "She's mad at me. I know why."

"You do?" Carole felt confused. "Why?"

"Because I messed up so much on Saturday. I wasn't listening well enough, and Veronica was trying to tell me what to do, and I couldn't do it. It's my fault Veronica fell off and it's my fault she's not in the drill anymore, and now she hates me. I'd hate me too if I couldn't be in the drill." Jessica's lower lip quivered. She obviously meant every word she said.

Carole ducked under Penny's head and put her hands on Jessica's shoulders. "You've got it all wrong, Jessica."

Jessica sniffed. "What's wrong?"

"All of it. You had nothing to do with Veronica getting thrown out of the drill. Veronica has been thrown out of all sorts of things without your help before, and this is no different. Besides, if you'll re-member, Max didn't say she couldn't be in it. All he said was that she didn't have to be in it. She's the one who decided that she didn't want to."

"But if she hadn't fallen off Garnet, she would have stayed in," Jessica argued. "And it was my fault that she fell off Garnet."

Carole suppressed the urge to tell Jessica that she thought Veronica had fallen off on purpose. Somehow

68

that didn't seem like the right sort of thing to tell a little girl. Plus, Carole didn't know for sure that it was true—she was only 99.9 percent sure that it was. Instead, she asked Jessica, "Have you ever fallen off a horse before?"

Jessica blinked. "Sure. Three times—once here at Pine Hollow, and twice at my old stable."

"How did it feel?"

"Scary, at first. Once my pony bucked, and everything swirled around, and I fell on my head."

"Did that hurt?"

"No. I was wearing a hard hat—you should always wear a hard hat, Carole."

"I know." Carole tried hard not to smile.

"Then I just felt silly, because I was sitting on the ground. And I didn't want it to happen again, but I wasn't really afraid."

"That's right," Carole said, "That's how most people feel. Do you want to know something?"

"What?"

"When you get to be a better rider, it doesn't mean you don't fall off. You have better balance, but you ride horses that aren't quite as well-trained and you ride over harder stuff—like out in the woods or over jumps. So you end up falling off just about as much as when you were first learning to ride."

69

"Really?" Jessica looked doubtful.

"Really." Carole leaned forward and whispered confidentially, "I fell off Starlight just last week."

"Did you really?"

"Yep. I think he must have been half asleep, because he just tripped over his own feet. I know I was half asleep, because I did a somersault right over his head. I was embarrassed, too, but I wasn't hurt. So the point is, Jessica, do you remember how Veronica landed when she fell?"

Jessica thought for a moment. "She was standing up, yelling at Max."

"That's right. How much do you think it hurt her to fall off and land on her feet?"

Jessica shook her head. "Probably not much."

"Probably you're right," Carole agreed. "And I guarantee you that I've seen Veronica come off many times before, and it usually doesn't make her stop riding. So that's the first point—Veronica didn't quit because she fell off. She quit because she was having a temper tantrum.

"That's the first point," Carole continued. "The second point is, it wasn't your fault that Veronica fell off anyway."

"Yes it was," Jessica persisted. "I kicked Penny and he ran into Garnet, and Garnet bucked."

70

"I remember," Carole said. "Did you run into Garnet on purpose?"

"No!" Jessica looked shocked.

"Then it wasn't your fault. Advanced riders are supposed to be ready for anything their horses do—if Garnet bucked, for whatever reason, Veronica should have been able to stay on. She would have, too, if she hadn't been so busy being angry about the drill. Do you know what I thought was really good about that whole incident, Jessica?"

"What?"

"It was that *you* stayed on. Penny moved sideways pretty quickly, and you not only stayed on her, you got her out of the way and back under control. That's really good riding. You're only a beginner, Jessica, but you've learned a lot and you should be proud of yourself. Don't be worried about what Veronica is up to—or down to. She's not worth it."

"Thanks, Carole, for trying to make me feel better," Jessica said. She gathered the grooming gear sadly, and Carole could tell that none of her words had really sunk in—Jessica still blamed herself.

"You rode really well today too," Carole said.

"I don't trot right," Jessica said. "Not in that middle crossing part."

"You almost got it today—I saw you," Carole said.

"Jessica, go easy on yourself. You're doing something difficult, and you haven't been riding long. You're doing well."

Tears welled up in Jessica's eyes again. "I'm so afraid I'm going to mess up," she whispered. "Carole, what if I don't get it right? I'll mess up the whole drill and no one will give money to CARL."

Carole gave her a hug. "You'll do great," she said. She watched Jessica trudge slowly down the aisle with Penny's gear and felt almost heartbroken. How could they help her? It seemed to Carole that Jessica was as lost and lonely as some of the animals Lisa had told her about from CARL.

FOUNDERS' DAY DAWNED bright and clear, and the first event on the program was the parade. Willow Creek was a suburb of Washington, D.C., but it had been around for a long time and had a lot of history and heritage of its own. Everyone in Willow Creek was proud of that heritage, and looked forward to celebrating it on Founders' Day. The parade route was lined with balloons and brightly colored flags—and people.

"Half of the town must be here watching," said Carole, looking down the street at the start of the parade. Sunlight shone off Starlight's gleaming neck and off the bright ribbons she'd braided into his mane. She loved days like this one.

"And the half that isn't watching is *in* the parade," Lisa agreed. Delilah didn't have the natural flair that Starlight had, but Lisa had groomed her thoroughly and her golden coat was beautiful. She rode next to Carole toward the rear of the Pine Hollow group. Max led off, with Red O'Malley and Mrs. Reg on either side, but most of the more advanced riders rode in the back. It was best to have them there, where they could keep an eye on the younger ones in front and be ready to help if trouble arose.

Next to Lisa, Belle pranced nervously and ogled a flapping flag. She arched her neck and began to snort. *"Belle,"* Stevie said sternly. Belle sighed, relaxed, and walked forward calmly.

"What was that about?" asked Lisa.

"She was just trying to get away with something," explained Stevie. "She wasn't actually afraid. She just needs to be told what her limits are."

Carole grinned. "Kind of like her rider?"

Stevie grinned back. "That's why we make such a terrific pair."

"Hey, Mom! Hi, Dad!" Lisa caught sight of her parents in the crowd and waved. They waved back to

74

Lisa excitedly. Colonel Hanson was standing only a few feet farther along the route, and they waved to him too.

"My parents will be closer to the judges' grandstand," Stevie said. "Chad's marching with the school band, and they want to hear him play." She made a face. "I don't know why they want to. We've been listening to him practice all week, and I promise you, I'd rather see him just march."

JUST AHEAD OF The Saddle Club, Veronica rode next to Jessica Adler. Even though Veronica wasn't in the drill and planned to take Garnet straight back to Pine Hollow after the parade, nothing would keep her from showing off her beautiful purebred mare. She smiled and waved to the crowd.

Jessica was feeling a little nervous. She wasn't quite used to riding outside of a fenced-in riding ring, and she'd never been in a parade before. All the people were looking at *her*. What if she messed up? Even though she wasn't afraid of falling, she was pretty sure that if she fell onto the asphalt road, it would hurt. And what if Penny ran off and got hurt? All sorts of dreadful possibilities crowded into Jessica's mind.

Just ahead, Jasmine and May were giggling and calling out to someone they knew on the sidelines. Jessica wished she could ride with them—then she might feel better. But Max had told Veronica to keep an eye on her, so she was stuck. She looked around for her parents. They were there somewhere, but she wasn't sure she'd be able to find them. So many people!

A small boy on the edge of the crowd threw a piece of popcorn at her. He grinned and waved, so she knew he didn't mean it badly, but the popcorn hit Penny on the nose. Penny tossed her head and pranced a few steps. Jessica clutched at the reins. Poor Penny! But what if she ran? What would she do? Unconsciously, Jessica tensed. Her legs gripped Penny hard.

Penny hadn't been upset by the popcorn, just surprised. She had been ridden in the Founders' Day parade for years. But when Jessica froze in terror on her back, Penny began to think that something was wrong. The pony began to be frightened too, and she tensed and grabbed at the bit.

"Make her stop that," said Veronica, looking down at Jessica. "Don't let her act like that. Sit up and use your legs."

Jessica sat up and gripped even harder. Penny began to trot.

"Stop her!" Veronica said. "Shorten your reins, Jessica! Don't let her act like that!"

Jessica shortened her reins and pulled. Penny came

76

back to a nervous, head-flinging walk. Jessica felt awful—she knew that something terrible was about to happen. Penny would run away. There was nothing she could do.

"UH-OH," SAID STEVIE. "Did you see that?" She broke away from Lisa and Carole and trotted Belle up to Veronica's side.

"See what?" asked Lisa. She had been waving to some of her friends from school.

Carole frowned. "Some kid threw something at Penny, and it made Jessica nervous. The more nervous Jessica gets, the more nervous Penny gets—"

"And the more nervous Penny gets, the more nervous Jessica gets," finished Lisa. "Poor kid. I remember how that feels." Lisa had been a beginner rider not long ago.

"Yeah," said Carole. "Veronica's been talking to her, but she's making things worse, not better." She shrugged and smiled at Lisa. "Stevie will fix it."

THERE WASN'T ROOM for Stevie to ride Belle in between Veronica and Jessica, so she was stuck on the outside of Garnet. But seeing how upset Veronica had made Jessica, Stevie was pretty sure she could improve the situation just by distracting Veronica.

77

"So," she said, "I suppose you've heard about our fortune-telling booth?"

"Not really," said Veronica. "I don't keep tabs on your affairs."

Oh, really! Stevie ground her teeth. She wished that just once she could say something like "tabs on your affairs" in that snooty voice Veronica used—only she'd say it *to* Veronica. Still, for Jessica and for the fortune-telling booth, Stevie kept her voice pleasant.

"We're having a Goodluck Horseshoe fortune-telling booth here at Founders' Day," she explained. "We're going to tell people their fortunes—anything they want to know, for the bargain price of only one dollar! That's cheap for fortunes these days," she added.

Veronica sniffed. "I'm not sure I'd be interested in a bargain fortune," she said.

"Oh, well," Stevie said cheerfully, "we'd be happy to charge you more."

Veronica looked skeptical. "Do you really know how to predict the future?"

"Oh, yes," Stevie assured her. "We've been reading books, studying charts, all kinds of things. The stars, palm-reading techniques, tea leaves. There's no end to what you can learn if you put your mind to it."

"Mmmm. And do your fortunes cover matters of the heart?"

" 'Matters of the heart?' " Stevie repeated. She couldn't help but notice that Veronica glanced back at Michael Grant as she spoke. Stevie's sides quivered; it was all she could do not to break into waves of hysterical laughter. But no, for the sake of the Good-luck Horseshoe she kept her mouth closed. "Sure," she said weakly. "We know all there is to know about matters of the heart."

Veronica smiled. "Maybe I'll pay your little booth a visit," she said. Then, looking again at Michael Grant and glancing quickly at Jessica to her side, Veronica asked, "Do you mind riding here, Stevie? I'd like to ride where I could have some interesting conversation."

"Be my guest," Stevie said. At least that would leave her alone with Jessica. Veronica dropped back a few rows—to Michael Grant's side. Stevie shook her head. Matters of the heart!

Without Veronica's interference, Jessica had succeeded in calming Penny down by talking to her soothingly. Her reins were still too tight and she was still nervous, but at least Penny wasn't fighting to trot.

"You seem to have her pretty well in hand," Stevie said to Jessica. "Try not to feel too nervous—I remem-

79

ber my first Founders' Day parade. I was riding Nickel, not Penny, and boy was I shaking! I know just how you're feeling."

Jessica smiled weakly. "I just don't ride well enough for this," she said. "I guess I shouldn't have come."

"What do you mean? You're doing fine!"

Jessica shook her head. "Veronica told me about thirty things I was doing wrong, and I didn't even know I was doing them wrong. And I'm sure Penny's going to run away."

"Don't ever listen to Veronica," Stevie told her firmly. "Listen to me instead. Max would never let anyone ride in the parade if he didn't think they were ready, and he let you, so you must be a good enough rider to do it. Penny's about twice as old as you and she likes parades. She's not going to run away. Just give her a pat and tell her she's okay."

Obediently Jessica bent to pat Penny's neck. In doing so, she automatically loosened the reins, and Penny stretched her neck out, relieved. "Good girl, Penny," Jessica said softly. Bending forward also made some of Jessica's tense muscles relax. Penny felt the change and relaxed even further.

"See?" said Stevie. "You just needed to tell her she's okay. Now I'll teach you my Stevie-Lake-riding-nervous-horses trick. Do you want to know it? It's a very special trick—I almost never share it with any-one."

"And you want to tell me?" Jessica's eyes were big.

"I'll share it with you, Jessica, because I can tell you're going to be a really good rider someday, and I want to be able to say that I helped you." Stevie bent toward Jessica. "The secret is: breathe."

"Breathe?" Jessica looked confused. "That's it?"

"That's it. Sounds amazing, but it works. Breathe great big deep breaths, the bigger and deeper the bet-ter. Your horse will calm right down. Guaranteed."

"It really works? Why?"

Stevie bent down again, looking mysterious. "I have no idea," she said solemnly. Jessica giggled. The parade was starting to be fun.

Stevie rode close to Jessica for the rest of the parade. As they passed the judges' grandstand, they formed up into even rows and columns and went by at a stately show walk. Stevie glanced to her side. Jessica was riding solemnly, her hands low and her chin held high. When she saw Stevie looking at her, she winked. Stevie grinned. Jessica would be okay.

AT THE END of the parade route, Horse Wise rode to a temporary corral on the fairgrounds that Max had set up for them. The drill wasn't until late afternoon, so this gave the horses a comfortable, shady place to stay while they waited.

"I can't stand Veronica," Stevie said as she began to untack Belle. "Every day she annoys me more and more. She had Jessica so upset, she could hardly ride." Stevie pulled some carrots out of the pocket of her show coat and fed one to her mare. She handed the rest to her friends to give to their horses too.

"We saw how you took care of her," said Carole. "Typical Stevie—in five minutes Veronica was gone and Jessica was laughing! It was great!"

"Yeah—and I even managed to put in a good word about our Goodluck Horseshoe booth." She repeated what Veronica had asked about "matters of the heart." Lisa and Carole covered their mouths and shrieked.

"Well," said Lisa, the first to recover, "I really wish we could do something permanent to help Jessica. I wish she had a friend near her home."

"Or a pet," said Carole.

"A big, friendly pet," agreed Lisa. "Hey!" Her face lit up. "Like maybe a big friendly dog that needs a lot of attention?"

Carole and Stevie stared at her.

"Yeah," said Stevie.

"Yeah," said Carole.

Stevie held up her hand. "Wait," she said. "I'm beginning to get an idea. . . ."

After a few minutes of planning, The Saddle Club returned to the task of making their horses comfortable. To their surprise, their three Pony Club "little sisters," Jessica, Jasmine, and May, came over to help.

"We know you're doing a fortune-telling booth," May announced. "You're probably in a hurry to go, so we thought we'd help you for a change." She went matter-of-factly to Lisa's side. "Want me to get Delilah some water?"

"Thanks," Lisa said. May grabbed a bucket and headed for the spigot.

Jessica took Starlight's lead rope from Carole. "I can tie him for you," she offered. "Remember, you showed me how."

With their help, The Saddle Club was soon ready to go. They headed for the parking lot on the other side of the grounds. They had packed Stevie's brother's tent and the rest of their gear into the back of Colonel Hanson's station wagon. Lisa pulled out the box of scarves and decorations. "Wow. This is heavier than it looks. Where should we set up?"

Stevie pointed. "How about there—right across

83

from the CARL booth?" Lisa and Carole exchanged grins.

"Perfect."

THEY PICKED OUT a great spot underneath a maple tree, not far from the van that had come from CARL. "Before we get set up, let's go see what the CARL booth is about," Stevie suggested. They piled the tent on top of their boxes and walked across the dirt road that separated their spot from CARL's van.

"Judy!" Carole was the first to recognize Judy Barker, the Pine Hollow vet, sitting in a chair near the van. Carole had been on rounds with Judy many times.

"Carole—and the rest of The Saddle Club!" Judy stood up, obviously glad to see them. "Did you enjoy riding in the parade?"

"Sure," said Stevie. "I think we'll enjoy this afternoon's drill even more. In the meantime, we're going to tell people's fortunes—we're donating the money to CARL."

Judy beamed. "That's a great idea," she said. "I'll be sure to steer customers your way."

"And we'll steer them yours," Lisa promised. "What's CARL doing here today?"

"Well, since your Pony Club is having the drill for

us, we thought we should be on hand to distribute literature about CARL and about animal care. I've brought along a few of our dogs and cats that are ready for adoption, too, in case we get some interested families."

"Trump?" Lisa asked excitedly.

"Yes, Trump, among others. Come say hello." She led The Saddle Club to the other side of the van, where a few traveling cages sat on the grass in the shade. Trump couldn't jump up and down inside his smaller cage, but he wagged his tail hard and wiggled his body. The Saddle Club petted him enthusiastically.

"He's wonderful," said Stevie. "How much would it cost to adopt him?"

Judy thought for a moment. "Our adoptive families don't have to pay for the animals," she said, "but we do require them to cover the cost of immunizing and neutering them. Trump's already been neutered. You could adopt him for twenty-five dollars. Are you looking for a dog, Stevie?"

"Just curious," Stevie said.

"Good luck with your fortunes," Judy called as they returned to their spot under the tree.

*   *   *

THE TENT TOOK only a few minutes to set up. "It's idiot-proof," Stevie said. "The only kind of tent my brother Chad could handle."

They covered their large cardboard box with a bright gauzy scarf to use as a table, and covered a smaller wooden box with a pink table-runner to use as a chair. Lisa hung a heavy patterned tablecloth behind the chair to make a screen, and Carole hung another similar cloth over the tent's door.

"This makes a better entrance," she explained. "It's much more mystical."

Meanwhile Stevie was hanging glittering cardboard stars and moons on the outside of the tent. Lisa and Carole unpacked the crystal ball, tea leaves, astrological charts, and playing cards. Finally, all three of them hung a large cardboard horseshoe above the entrance, and put up a sign reading GOODLUCK HORSESHOE FORTUNE-TELLING BOOTH. YOUR FUTURE REVEALED TO YOU. $1.00. Underneath that Lisa hung a smaller sign reading PROCEEDS TO BENEFIT CARL.

Lisa, Carole, and Stevie stepped back to admire their booth. It was perfect. Lisa smiled at her friends. "We're in business!" she said.

9

INSIDE THE TENT, Stevie dressed in the fortune-teller's flowing robe—actually Lisa's mother's second-best bathrobe—earrings, and purple scarf. "Do you really think this is going to work?" Lisa asked her.

"Of course it is," Stevie assured her. "We're the ones who know the future!"

"I know what you mean," Lisa said. "But this is a little weird."

"Lisa. You've got to have faith. By the end of the day"—Stevie waved her hand mysteriously—"everyone's problems will be solved!"

Since Stevie was taking the first stint as fortune-teller, Carole and Lisa began walking through the fairgrounds, drumming up business for the booth. "Fortunes read!" they cried. "Get your fortunes read! Learn the secrets of your future! Visit the Goodluck Horseshoe fortune-telling booth! Only one dollar!"

Stevie didn't have long to wait before the first visitor ducked his head to enter the tent. It was Colonel Hanson.

"Hello, stranger," Stevie said in her most mysterious tones.

"Hello, Madame. Here's your dollar." Colonel Hanson sat down on the box on the other side of the table. "Let me have your best shot."

Stevie spread her deck of playing cards out in front of her. "Hmmm, a black seven and a queen of diamonds," she murmured. "And here's the three of spades." She looked up. "The cards tell me you love old movies," she said.

"Amazing," said Colonel Hanson. "You can tell that from those cards?"

"Particularly old movies about the Marines."

Colonel Hanson slapped his forehead. "You don't say!"

"Certainly!"

"Amazing—your prowess is incredible."

"Wait," said Stevie, "there's more—I'm getting something—very strong signals—" She cupped both hands around her father's paperweight. "Yes. I can see that you have a finely developed sense of humor. And excellent taste in old jokes."

"Finely developed or not, Madame Fortune-Teller, you're going to have to do better than this for the buck I just paid you. Tell me something about my future."

Stevie stared at the paperweight for a long time. She couldn't very well make up a future for Carole's father. Finally she knew what to say. "You're going to be very proud of your daughter," she predicted.

Colonel Hanson laughed, but seemed to appreciate his fortune. "I'd say that will certainly be true," he said. "I'm already proud of her. Okay, Madame Fortune, you've earned your dollar." He rose to go, but paused at the tent's door. "And, Stevie—good luck!"

Stevie sighed with relief as she put his dollar into her pocket. Fortune-telling was hard. I'm going to have to do better than that, she thought, if I'm going to fool anyone.

Her next customer was Max. Stevie swirled some soggy tea leaves in a cup. "You love horses," she said.

"That's right—but did you know that from the tea leaves or because I'm wearing breeches?" Max grinned, and Stevie grinned back. He had just given her a valuable hint. She asked Max his birthday, and consulted her astrological chart. "I'm a Pisces," Max added. "If that helps."

"Ahh—the sign of the fish," said Stevie. "Definitely there are fish in your future—fish dinner? Goldfish? Have you eaten fish recently, stranger?"

Max shook his head.

"No, I have it!" cried Stevie. "You'll be taking a sea voyage sometime soon!" She remembered the cruise brochures she had seen on Max's desk—she was pretty sure he'd been planning his honeymoon. "A long, happy voyage," she added.

"And your heartline crosses your byline," she continued, examining his palm. "There are words in your future—words and romance." Max was engaged to marry a reporter named Deborah Hale.

"Very nice," Max said, taking his hand back. "An excellent future." On his way out the door, he told the next customer, "She seemed to know everything about me!"

After that Stevie told fortunes to several strangers. She found that not knowing the person made telling their fortunes much easier, and she began to enjoy herself.

First a small boy came in who looked like he'd recently been in a fight—maybe even that morning. His jeans were ripped and his shirt was stained, and he had a swollen lip that had recently been bleeding.

"You're stronger than you look," Stevie said, examining his grubby hand.

"Yeah?" The boy looked interested.

"Definitely. And you're not a coward—you'll never be a coward." She consulted her crystal ball. "Hmmm. But I see a better way to resolve problems. You must learn a better way."

"I should?"

"Hmmm. Yes. Try to talk things out instead of fighting. If you do, your rewards will be great."

"Will I get money?" asked the boy.

"Great rewards," Stevie repeated. "Like, maybe you won't get grounded so often."

"Wow!" said the boy.

THE NEXT CUSTOMER was a shy little girl who looked like she was hiding behind the hair that hung in front of her face.

"Come closer," Stevie beckoned in a trancelike voice, "do not be afraid."

The girl crept closer. Stevie turned over a few of the playing cards. "You will be beautiful when you grow up," she said.

91

The little girl stared at her. "Beautiful and strong," Stevie said. "You will be able to do anything you try to do. Don't be afraid to try."

"YOU'LL LEARN TO ride horses," she predicted to a tiny girl wearing an oversize I'D RATHER BE RIDING T-shirt. "You'll love horses your whole life."

"Just like my mommy?" asked the little girl.

"Just like her," Stevie said.

"YOU'LL TRAVEL TO exotic places," she told a teenage girl who definitely looked bored with Willow Creek.

"THE COMING YEAR will bring you much joy," she said to a young pregnant woman, who left smiling.

"WHAT DO YOU want to know about your future?" she asked the next customers, a pair of boys her brother Michael's age.

"Will our Little League team win the championship?" one asked.

Stevie considered the question over her charts and tea leaves. "If you finish with the best record, you'll certainly win the championship," she said. "But if you don't, there's always next year."

I hope they don't think too hard about that one, she told herself as they left.

AND THEN CAME the moment Stevie had been waiting for. Veronica entered the tent. "Come, come!" Stevie said, gesturing grandly. "Sit and have your fortune told!"

"I'm not sure I believe in this stuff." Veronica sat and handed Stevie a crisp dollar bill from her leather purse.

"Let me see your palm," Stevie murmured, taking Veronica's right hand and turning it over. "Such a nice palm too. Smooth skin, no calluses, a beautiful and expensive manicure. I can see you lead a life of leisure. It will be a pleasure to read the future from a palm like this. What do you particularly want to know?"

"Oh, come on," said Veronica. "You can't fool me, Stevie." But she didn't pull her hand away.

"Strong lifelines and heartlines," Stevie said as if she hadn't heard Veronica. "Definitely a lot of money has come through this hand. I can see you're a person of taste and experience, a person who enjoys the finer things in life. But you must tell me, what do you want to know?"

Veronica twisted in her seat, but Stevie's flattery

had begun to sway her. Finally she said, "I want to know about matters of the heart."

"Matters of the heart. Of course you do." Stevie dropped Veronica's hand and leaned backward, half closing her eyes and assuming a trancelike state. "Mmmm-ummm-oommm. I see it—I see him. The man of your dreams is before me. I see him, the perfect match for you. Tall, but not too tall. Good teeth. Wavy brown hair, nice brown eyes, a straight nose, and thin yet sensuous lips. I see him riding a horse. I see him here at Founders' Day today. He's new to this area. I see him—no, he's fading . . . fading—" Stevie shook her head and appeared to wake up from her trance. "Whew! That was strong! It fades in and out, you know—like a bad radio station. Did I say anything that made sense to you?"

Veronica was staring at her open-mouthed. "You described Michael Grant," she said. "It sounded exactly like him."

"Really? Imagine that!"

"Go on," said Veronica. "Tell me more."

Stevie shook her head. "That's all you get for one dollar," she said. "You're welcome to come back later if you want to hear some more." She closed her eyes firmly until she heard Veronica leave the tent.

"All clear," she whispered. Carole and Lisa burst

94

out from behind the back curtain. They'd come in through the back tent flap after walking twice around the fairgrounds.

"You were great!" Lisa said.

"Did you hear everything I said to Veronica?"

"Every word," Carole confirmed. "It couldn't have gone better! Operation Fix Everything is on its way!"

Now it was Lisa's turn to be the fortune-teller. She donned the robe, scarf, and earrings, and rearranged the props on the top of the table.

"What were you doing with the cards?" she asked Stevie.

"Shuffling them, really. Like you're dealing out a poker hand."

"I never dealt a poker hand."

"Don't worry about the cards. Want some fresh tea leaves?"

Lisa laughed. "After walking twice around the grounds, what I'd like is a soda! Shh—someone's coming!"

Stevie and Carole ducked behind the curtain. Lisa adjusted the shoulders of her robe and thought about the way a fortune-teller should speak. She loved acting, and she knew quite a lot about it. She'd even played the lead role in a community theater production of *Annie*. The customers paused nervously outside the door. Lisa could hear them shuffling.

"Come in!" she commanded imperiously. "The Horseshoe calls you!"

Behind the curtain Stevie and Carole stifled their giggles. The Saddle Club was off to a fantastic start!

THE SHUFFLING AT the tent flap stopped, and two little girls peered inside. May and Jasmine.

"Come in!" Lisa said in sweeping tones, motioning them forward with her arm. "Don't be afraid," she added because both of them looked a little scared.

"We want to know something," said May. "We have a question for you."

"You can ask the crystal ball whatever you like," Lisa said, pointing to the paperweight.

"We'd rather ask you," May replied.

"That works too," Lisa said.

"Does Joey Dutton really have to leave?" Jasmine asked. "Because he says he isn't going unless he has to,

97

and we don't want him to go, and we want to know if he really does have to."

Lisa knew that Joey Dutton, one of Horse Wise's youngest members, lived near Jasmine and May. She also knew that Joey's dad was moving his dental practice to the town where Stevie's boyfriend, Phil Marsten, lived. "Are you guys good friends with Joey?" she asked them.

"He's our best friend!" said May. "We play at his house all the time, and he comes over and plays with us, and he's got a tree fort and everything. And now he's riding, and he's going to get a pony and he was going to keep it in his backyard like we do. Everything was going to be perfect, but now he's moving away!"

Lisa knew that nothing she said would keep Joey from moving. "He has to go with his family," she told Jasmine and May, "but I can promise you that you'll still get to see him often."

"We will?" Jasmine asked excitedly.

"Of course we will," May answered. "He'll be in the Cross County Pony Club instead, and we'll see him every time Horse Wise and Cross County have a competition. We didn't need a fortune-teller to tell us that."

Lisa could tell she was going to have to do better. "Mmm," she murmured, waving her hands over the deck of playing cards. She pulled a card from the pile. "See here, this is the two of spades," she said, "and spades is trump." Lisa didn't know what "trump" meant in cards, but she had heard her mother saying it when she played bridge. "This is a very lucky sign," Lisa said solemnly. "It means that even without Joey you two are going to have a wonderful summer."

"Wow," said Jasmine. Even May seemed impressed. They paid up and left satisfied. Lisa could hear Jasmine repeat "Spades is trump" under her breath as she went out the door. Lisa hoped there weren't any bridge players standing in line.

She had three more customers, all younger kids who seemed pleased with the fortunes she told them. Of course, Lisa reflected, who wouldn't be pleased to hear "Your grades will improve," "Your allowance will increase soon," and "You will meet a dark, handsome stranger"?

Then in came Michael Grant!

With her finest gestures Lisa bade him to be seated. She inhaled deeply and mysteriously and stared at him for several seconds. "Do you know your sign?" she asked him in a deep and mysterious voice.

"Sign?" Michael looked puzzled.

"Sign," Lisa repeated. "Like, the sign you were born under."

Michael thought hard. "I don't think there was a sign," he said.

Lisa sighed. "Like, Gemini, that's one of the signs," she said. She didn't know all of the zodiac signs herself, but she knew that "What's your sign?" was considered a very good question for fortune-tellers to ask. Except, of course, when the person you asked didn't know what you were talking about.

"I rode a roller coaster called Gemini once," Michael offered. "But that was three years ago."

"That counts," Lisa said. "Let me consult my charts." She made a big show of checking the astrological charts Stevie had photocopied from an encyclopedia. "Very favorable," she said. "I can see that Mercury is rising in—umm—your thermometer, and the moon is pretty far from a solar eclipse. Very favorable signs, indeed."

She turned and gave Michael another long and very effective look. He shifted slightly in his seat. "I think I can answer a question for you, Michael. You may ask the crystal ball. What is it you would like to know?"

Michael pointed at the paperweight. "Is this the crystal ball?"

"Of course. Ask, and you shall be answered."

Michael bent low toward the crystal ball. Lisa bent

100

low, too, so that she could hear his question. Glancing cautiously at Lisa, Michael whispered, "Is she the one for me?"

Lisa bit her lip and assumed the trancelike state that Stevie had used with Veronica. "Let me see," she murmured. "Yes, yes, I'm getting something. The image of the girl of your dreams. The perfect girl for you —the one ordained by the stars . . ."

Lisa thought quickly. Who was that super model Stevie's brothers were always mooning over? "Your dream girl is beautiful in every way," she intoned. "Very tall and slender, with curving hips and a wonderful figure. Thick honey-blond hair, fair skin, wide brown eyes, a tiny mole on one cheek. Long, luxurious eyelashes. She's the one for you."

Lisa opened her eyes slowly. Michael looked a little stunned. Lisa's description didn't sound at all like Veronica diAngelo. "Are you sure that's right?" he asked. "I mean, it's not the answer I was expecting. Are you sure she's supposed to be a blonde?"

"Definitely," Lisa said. "I know exactly what I'm talking about, and this is the perfect girl for you. The crystal ball never lies!" She flung her arms out dramatically, reflecting that what she had said was indeed true. She was sure that Michael, just like Stevie's brothers, would love to go out with Cindy Crawford.

"Okay," Michael said, putting down his dollar. "Thanks for the info."

He left, and in came Jessica. She stood by the door looking shy and frightened.

"Come in," Lisa said very gently. "What would you like to know?"

"Oh," Jessica said. "I don't have any questions. I just thought it would be—fun—to know my future." She sat and looked down at her lap and then up at Lisa trustingly. "Things have been difficult," she said in a voice that hardly sounded like a little girl's. "I thought maybe you could tell me if they were going to get better."

Lisa's heart went out to her. Luckily, she knew just what to say. She turned over a few of the cards, had Jessica swirl the cup of wet tea leaves, and consulted her charts with great seriousness. "First of all," she said, "I can tell that you have a great future with horses. You're a good rider now, and all you have to do is keep practicing and learning. You'll be very good someday."

"Really?" Jessica looked amazed. She smiled into the cup of tea leaves.

"Really," Lisa repeated. "Also, I can see that you're going to get a new best friend from an unexpected

102

source. This friend is going to need your help, your love, and your attention."

This time Jessica seemed doubtful. She twisted her hands together. "Who wants to be my friend?" she asked Lisa at last. "No one does—not really."

Lisa felt like hugging Jessica, but she didn't want to give Jessica any reason to doubt her. She looked at the charts again. "I see a friend," she insisted. "You'll have to wait. Patience will bring you a special friend."

Jessica shrugged and smiled. "Okay." She left looking a lot happier than she had come in. Lisa smiled; that part had gone well.

The next customer was Veronica, back for more! Lisa could hardly believe her luck.

"I want to know everything else you can tell me," Veronica demanded, taking a seat on the box.

"Ummm." Lisa picked up her cards and shuffled them several times. She spread them out before her, facedown, and flipped a few over, and then back. "When were you born?" she asked suddenly. "What was the exact hour?"

Veronica frowned. "Three A.M."

Lisa pulled some of the cards out and set them aside. She reshuffled the remaining cards several times. Veronica began to look impatient. Lisa shuffled again and spread the cards out before her in a different direction. "What county was the hospital in?" she demanded.

"What hospital?"

"The hospital in which you were born." Lisa frowned and tried to look superior.

"Loudon County. Look, I don't see what that has to do with anything. All I want to know is about Michael Grant."

Lisa pretended not to hear Michael's name. "The county is very important," she said sternly. "I'm beginning to get a picture of your ideal man. He has come before—I have seen him before." Like about five minutes ago, Lisa said to herself.

"Really?" Veronica leaned forward. "What was he like?"

"You've already been told that," Lisa said to her.

Veronica smiled—she hadn't expected Lisa to know that. How could she, Lisa realized, when she didn't know that Carole and I were listening to Stevie's fortunes? "Very true," Veronica said, relaxing a little bit. "What else can you tell me about him?"

Lisa looked dreamily into the crystal paperweight. "I can see his tastes," she said. "I know what he likes and dislikes."

"Now we're getting somewhere," Veronica said. "Tell me."

"He's a simple man with simple needs," she said. "He's looking for a natural girl with simple tastes, without fancy airs. He doesn't like makeup or"—Lisa struggled to find the right words—"excess personal adornments." She smiled mystically at Veronica. As usual, Veronica was wearing lipstick and plenty of eye makeup. She had changed from the riding gear she had worn in the parade and was now wearing a pair of tailored and very expensive-looking linen shorts with a sleek silk blouse, large extravagant gold earrings, and leather flats. She'd managed to redo her hair too, and not a wisp was out of place.

"The man who came before dislikes hair spray," Lisa said firmly. "He likes a natural look, clean, sun-dried hair and a clean, well-scrubbed face. The man who came before wants a girl who is comfortable in blue jeans."

"Blue jeans?" Veronica asked. "He wants me to wear blue jeans?"

"He admires girls who wear blue jeans. He prefers old jeans—old jeans with holes and patches. He likes girls in tattered sweatshirts, old T-shirts, and well-worn, comfortable clothing."

Lisa could hardly keep from laughing. She couldn't remember ever having seen Veronica in jeans, unless they were brand-new neatly pressed designer jeans, and Veronica certainly never wore clothes with holes in them. Lisa had described someone who was the exact opposite of Veronica in every outward way.

"He does?"

"He does. His ideal girl does not wear jewelry or other expensive—er—trappings."

"And he was just in here, right?" Veronica pointed to the tent door.

"The man," Lisa replied, "has just come before."

Veronica looked surprised but satisfied. "Well, at least I know what I need to do." She began to get up from her seat.

"Wait!" Lisa flung her hands into the air. "I'm getting one thing more!"

"Yes?" Veronica spun around.

"No," said Lisa, "it's too important. It's going to cost you more than a dollar."

Veronica reached into her purse, but Lisa shook her head. "It's gone," she said, waving her hand near her forehead. "I wasn't concentrating, and it slipped away. Come back in a little while and we'll try again. I know it was very important."

Veronica looked unhappy. "Just so you're sure you can get it back," she said. "I don't want to miss anything important."

106

"I know we can," Lisa assured her. "It's a simple case of mind over matter." She began to reshuffle her cards.

Veronica slunk out the door. Lisa let out a sigh. "She's gone," she said. Stevie and Carole rolled out from behind the back flap, laughing.

"You were wonderful." Carole got up to hug Lisa and Stevie patted her on the back. "Even better than the time before!"

"I think she's buying it," Stevie said. "I really think she's buying it."

"Oh, she's definitely buying it," Lisa replied. "You should have seen her face! She nodded after everything I said—I'm surprised she didn't take notes!"

"Here." Stevie handed Lisa a soda. "Judy Barker saw us sitting back there and brought us these." Lisa took a grateful sip.

"A toast," Carole offered. "To the perfect setup for Project Fix Everything!" They raised their sodas in the air.

"And a toast to the Goodluck Horseshoe," said Lisa. "Look at all the money we've made!" She pulled out the envelope she was keeping under the table. "Some of the grown-ups even gave us more than a dollar."

"Wow. CARL is going to be thrilled," Stevie predicted.

"If only the rest of it goes well—"

"It'll go well," said Carole. "Now take off that robe. It's my turn!"

11

FOR THE NEXT forty-five minutes there was a line of customers waiting at the Goodluck Horseshoe tent. Inside, Carole was kept busy sloshing tea leaves and waving cards around. She predicted good weather, straight-A report cards, long sea voyages, new boyfriends, and, in one case, that the New York Mets would win the pennant.

Finally, Carole's big moment arrived. Veronica returned for the third time.

She had been transformed. Instead of the stylish, expensive clothes she had been wearing before, she now wore tattered blue jeans and a battered red Ralph Lauren sweatshirt. Looking closely, Carole could tell that the designer jeans weren't really old—the holes were new and clean-edged. It looked like Veronica had attacked them with scissors. The rips on the sweatshirt seemed new too. Veronica's fancy earrings were gone, her face was scrubbed clean, and her hair had been tied back in a plain tight ponytail.

Carole was thrilled.

Veronica hesitated at the door. "I was expecting Lisa," she said. "She promised to tell me more."

"We're all on the same wavelength," Carole assured her. "I'll be able to tell you exactly what you need to know." She held out her hand, and Veronica paid her another dollar.

Carole crossed her hands in front of her and began to hum. She hummed louder and louder, closing her eyes and leaning backward. Veronica waited.

"Yes," said Carole. "I understand what you need to know. You're looking for a clue to the heart of the man who came before."

"That's right," said Veronica. "I had the chauffeur take me home so I could change my clothes. What else do I need to do?"

"Hmmm." Carole swept her hands over the crystal ball, back and forth, several times. The motion seemed to transfix Veronica, who watched her closely.

"I see the key to his heart," Carole announced. "The man who came before wants a generous soul."

"Generous?"

"Yes. How much money do you have with you?"

Veronica looked into her purse. "I just got my allowance, but I spent some of it," she said. "Looks like twenty-eight dollars."

"You must take that money," said Carole, "and give it generously to a person in need."

"Wouldn't ten dollars be enough?" asked Veronica. "I was planning to buy some new lipstick—" Her voice dropped off, and Carole could see her wondering if she needed lipstick, since "the man who came before" didn't approve of makeup.

"No way," Carole told her. "It must be the whole twenty-eight."

Veronica blinked. "Anything else?" she asked. Carole shook her head. "Okay. Thanks for the help." She stumbled out of the tent, looking for a person in need.

Carole peeked out of the tent to watch. Just across from their booth, Stevie was introducing Jessica and Jessica's mother to Judy Barker. Judy was explaining to Mrs. Adler that CARL put many animals up for adoption.

"Oh, couldn't we get one?" Jessica begged, pulling on her mother's hand. "Can't we get a dog, Mom?"

"I know a great dog you could have," Stevie said. She looked over and saw Veronica come out of the booth, and her eyes widened. "For only twenty-five dollars," she added loudly.

"But I don't have twenty-five dollars," Jessica replied.

Veronica's head jerked around to look at Jessica. She stared for a moment, her hand going slowly to her purse, then she shook her head and looked away.

There, on the other side of the road, Lisa stood talking to Michael Grant. Lisa broke off the conversation and waved. "Hi, Veronica," she said. "Michael just told me he was looking for you."

"I did?" asked Michael. "I mean—sure I did."

Meanwhile, Stevie was saying to Jessica, "I couldn't hear you. What did you just say?"

"I said, I DON'T HAVE TWENTY-FIVE DOLLARS," Jessica shouted.

Veronica looked at Michael, who looked at Veronica, who looked back toward Jessica. The Saddle Club held their breaths.

"Here," Veronica said, pulling the wad of money out of her purse and handing it to Jessica, "why don't you get yourself a dog. There's enough there for you to buy it a toy or something too."

Jessica's mother shook her head. "That really isn't necessary," she said. "We can well afford—"

Veronica held up her hand. When she wanted to, she could be polite, and she was gracious now. "Please allow me to give Jessica a little present," she said. "She was my 'little sister,' you know, until I decided not to ride in the drill."

"Oh, thank you!" Jessica said. She threw her arms around Veronica's waist.

"Well, thank you, but I really don't think it's necessary," Jessica's mother said. "It's very nice of you, I'm sure."

Veronica pushed Jessica away gently and held up her hand again. "Please let me," she repeated. "It's such a pleasure for me to do things for others."

Jessica's mother looked at Jessica's ecstatic face and Veronica's earnest one. "Well," she said, "I know my daughter would really love a dog, and we'd like her to have one. Thank you very much."

"Thank you, Veronica!" Jessica waved happily as Veronica crossed the road to Michael's side. Lisa silently went back to the entrance of the tent.

"Can you believe that just happened?" she asked Carole. "It's exactly like a play."

"Keep watching," Carole replied, "It isn't over yet."

"She wanted me to have a dog," Jessica said to

113

Stevie, looking with wonder at the money Veronica had given her. "She must not hate me after all. She must *like* me."

"Of course she likes you," Stevie said.

"Then she must not think I'm a terrible rider either."

Stevie put her arm around the little girl's shoulder. "Nobody thinks you're a terrible rider," she said, "because you aren't. Come on. Do you want to meet the dog I was telling you about?" She led Jessica to the other side of the trailer.

"Hello, Michael," Veronica said silkily. "Did you see what I just did?"

"I sure did," Michael said, staring at her with a slightly disgusted expression. "I couldn't believe it."

"Oh, I do things like that all the time," Veronica said with a casual wave of her hand. "Money means so little to me."

"And what happened to your clothes?" he asked. "That's not what I saw you wearing earlier."

Veronica laughed, and touched his arm lightly. "Who wants to wear those fancy clothes all the time! I went home and changed. I'm much more comfortable dressed like this. They're much more like me— I'm sure you know what I mean. How do you like them?"

Michael swallowed hard and didn't answer. "I'd better go," he said. "Boy, you sure gave that little girl a lot of money. How much do you have left?"

"Nothing," Veronica replied proudly. "I gave her every cent I had."

Michael looked at her as if she'd just sprouted a second head. "I've really got to go," he stammered. "There's some blond girl I'm supposed to be looking for." He walked off shaking his head, Veronica trailing raggedly in his wake.

"Ohhh!" Carole and Lisa heard Jessica's cry of delight coming from the far side of CARL's van.

"Come on!" Lisa grabbed her friend's arm. "We don't want to miss this!" They ran across the road, Carole's fortune-teller's robe flapping in the wind.

Jessica was kneeling beside Trump's cage, her face pressed close to the wire. Trump was licking her furiously through the bars. "He's perfect!" She turned when The Saddle Club approached. "Do you want to meet my new dog?" she asked them. "His name's Buddy, I'm going to call him Buddy."

"He's an awfully nice dog," Lisa said. Carole felt that she could hardly speak.

"He's the *best* dog. Of course," Jessica added importantly, "Dr. Barker told me he isn't trained yet. I'm going to have to teach him everything."

Jessica's mother finished signing the adoption papers that Judy Barker had given her. Judy brought out a leash and carefully clipped it to Trump's—Buddy's—collar before opening the cage door. She handed the leash to Jessica. "Here you go. He's all yours."

Buddy bounded out of the cage and threw himself at Jessica. Jessica laughed and rolled with him on the grass. "Buddy, Buddy," she called. Then she stood up. "You can't jump up and down," she told him firmly. "You have to sit." She pressed down on Buddy's rear end and he sat, wagging his tail. "Good boy!" Buddy jumped up and licked Jessica's face. Jessica laughed again. "I think it will take a little while," she said to The Saddle Club. "But I know he'll learn."

Carole caught Stevie's and Lisa's arms. "Back to the booth," she said. "I've got fortunes to tell!"

"Forget the booth," Stevie said as they walked away. "We're done. We've accomplished all our goals—"

"First," said Lisa, "we've made oodles of money for CARL—"

"Second," said Stevie, "we've played a great joke on Veronica. She'll wear torn blue jeans for days."

"Third, we convinced Michael Grant to go searching for Cindy Crawford instead of Veronica. Not only

116

is that part of the joke on Veronica, it's no more than he deserves for wanting to go out only with rich girls."

"And fourth, and most important—not to mention miraculous," Lisa said, looking back at CARL's van, "we made Jessica very happy."

"You've forgotten the fifth thing," said Carole.

"Fifth thing? What's that?"

"We'd have to close down the booth anyway. It's almost time for our drill!"

They hurried to remove the signs from their tent. Luckily, it seemed that everyone who wanted their fortune told had already been there—no one else was waiting for them. Then they used the tent to change back into their riding gear.

"If we ride as well as we tell fortunes," Stevie said, "this drill will be fantastic!"

"THE HORSE WISE drill-team demonstration will begin in fifteen minutes in the west arena," a voice announced over the fairground's P.A. system. "Please come to the west arena for a drill-team demonstration."

Lisa hurriedly packed the scarves and tablecloth into a box while Carole and Stevie took down the tent. "Fifteen minutes! We haven't got much time!"

Judy Barker was loading the adoptive animals back into CARL's van. "You can put your stuff in here for now if you want to," she offered. "I'm going to move to the arena and set up there. I want everyone who comes to know about CARL."

The girls put their boxes into the van and helped Judy put the rest of her things inside. Judy drove them to the edge of the corral before going on to park at the arena. The girls thanked her and hurried out.

Their saddles and bridles were stacked neatly on the ground near Max's horse trailer. They hurried to gather them and their grooming buckets—the horses would be dusty after standing so long in the corral.

Almost all of the other riders were already there. "What took you so long?" May asked them. "You didn't forget about the drill, did you?"

"Of course not," Carole said, patting Starlight gently before beginning to groom him. "You knew we wouldn't. Is Jessica here?"

"Yes, she's almost ready. Guess who isn't here, though? You'll never guess." May shifted her weight from one foot to the other and grinned. "In fact, he told Max he didn't think he really wanted to be part of Horse Wise. He quit! It was Michael Grant!"

"Really?" Stevie straightened from checking Belle's feet. "That's weird—I wonder why he quit."

"I don't know," said May. "Maybe Veronica was bugging him too much. She's been following him around. But I don't care if he's gone, because it makes us even again, and that's a lot easier for the drill." Stevie knew what she meant. With an odd number of

119

riders in the drill, the one unpaired person always looked like a leftover.

Stevie grinned. "I guess I won't miss him."

"Nope." May went back to Macaroni, and The Saddle Club finished tacking up their horses.

"How do I look?" Carole asked.

Lisa tucked a stray wisp of hair behind her friend's left ear. Even after hurrying in the dusty weather, Carole's show clothes and boots were immaculate. "Great."

"We'd better mount up," Stevie said. "I can see Max getting ready to make an announcement."

They swung into their saddles and rode out of the corral. Outside the arena they got into line in the order in which they would begin the drill. A good-size crowd had gathered in the stands, and The Saddle Club could see Judy standing outside the van with its large banner reading COUNTY ANIMAL RESCUE LEAGUE, talking briskly and handing out brochures. When Max carried a microphone into the center of the arena, the crowd quieted.

"Welcome," he said. "I'm glad to see so many people here today for the Horse Wise drill-team demonstration. There's no charge for this event, but afterward, if you've enjoyed watching, we hope you'll make a donation to CARL, the County Animal Rescue League.

"Horse Wise is a local Pony Club based at my stable, Pine Hollow, right here in Willow Creek. Our members vary widely in age and riding experience, and you'll see most of them performing in the drill today. These young riders have worked very hard for the past few weeks on this drill, and I think you'll find they've put their efforts to good use.

"The County Animal Rescue League has been putting their efforts to good use for several years here in Willow Creek. I'm sure that most of you are familiar with the work they do, but if not, please stop by the van parked near the entrance to the arena for more information after the drill."

Max paused and Stevie thought she saw him smile in their direction. "Today a few of my riders forecast good futures for some of you here at the fair. After our drill I hope that you will all help see to it that the animals at CARL have good futures too."

Max strode out of the arena and the music began. *Bump-ba-da-da-dum-dum, bump-ba-da-da-dum-dum.* Waiting at the gate, Stevie counted slowly under her breath; next to her, she could hear Jackie counting too. At the exact right moment, at the exact same

121

time, they signaled their horses and cantered into the ring.

Lisa had been against the idea of starting the drill at the canter. It was flashy, it caught the audience's attention from the start, and it fit perfectly with the start of the music, but it was difficult for some of the riders to make their horses canter exactly on cue—starting at the walk or trot was much less risky. Now, waiting her turn at the back of the line, Lisa was glad that she'd been overruled. The horses were behaving well and everyone was riding perfectly. The cantering start looked fantastic.

Carole hadn't forgotten her earlier trouble with the paired circles. Now, even though Starlight was performing beautifully, she didn't let herself get caught up admiring him, or let the thousand little movements that made up every larger movement distract her from the drill as a whole. She kept her ear tuned toward the music and tried to help Starlight move with it. She remembered the whole sequence of the drill, and more important, she remembered to watch her "little sister" out of the corner of her eye. She kept Starlight's movements on scale with Outlaw's.

Jasmine, too, was helping Outlaw move as largely and expressively as he could so that his gaits would more closely equal Starlight's. They completed their circles perfectly this time—round and even, and exactly half a circle apart. We've learned to work together, Carole realized. We've really become a team.

Stevie had not wanted to admit to anyone that she had been nervous about Belle. She loved her horse devotedly, and she had always felt that they made a terrific pair—that Belle listened and responded to her and that they trusted each other. But Belle was still new enough to Stevie that she hadn't been sure how the mare would respond to the commotion of the parade and public performance. Practicing in the ring at Pine Hollow was one thing, but this was quite another. Stevie's old mount, Topside, had been a champion show horse, and she always knew that he loved crowds.

Now, to Stevie's delight, Belle was showing the same sort of response that Stevie would have expected from Topside. The crowd had seemed to make her more alert, yet steadier—she waited for Stevie's commands as if she sensed their extra-special importance. And Stevie couldn't help but feel that her horse was trying to show off. Surely Belle had never arched her neck so elegantly or strutted so proudly before!

Movement by movement the drill progressed. Finally they reached the cross through the center. Carole thought of Jessica, and her heart constricted. So much had gone right for Jessica today—could she pull this off too? Carole remembered how close Jessica had come in their last practice. She didn't dare turn her head to see Jessica start, but as soon as she and Starlight were through their corner she looked sideways to the center of the ring.

Jessica was crossing through the center with a gigantic smile on her face. Penny, little Penny, was absolutely flying—trotting with enormous groundswallowing strides that kept her right on speed without breaking gait! They'd done it! Carole wanted to cheer. But she turned her eyes forward and her attention resolutely back to the next part of the drill. They'd all done so well—she didn't want to mess up now.

As the final strains of music ended, the riders halted squarely in a row facing the grandstand. To their surprise, the audience erupted into applause. Even Max looked elated. "That was better than our best practice!" he told them as they rode out of the arena. "Am I proud of you!"

"Am I proud of you!" echoed Stevie. She dismounted and flung her arms around Belle's neck. The mare turned her head and drooled on Stevie's jacket.

Carole and Lisa felt the same way. They also dismounted and gave their horses plenty of pats and hugs. The other riders did the same. They were all thrilled with their success.

Carole walked Starlight over to where the little girls were chattering excitedly. "Great job, all of you!" she said.

"Thanks!" chorused May and Jessica.

"Thanks," said Jasmine. "You did pretty well too, Carole, on those circles." She grinned mischievously.

"I guess Outlaw can keep up with Starlight," Carole agreed, grinning back. "At least, that is, when you ride him that well."

Jessica and Jasmine laughed, but May grew indignant. "Outlaw's nothing special compared to Starlight," she said. "Starlight's beautiful."

"Outlaw's beautiful too," Jasmine defended him staunchly. "He's the best pony ever."

"Jasmine's right," Carole said, trying to calm them down before they really started to argue. "And how about you, Jessica? You had Penny really moving out there."

Jessica's face shone. "I just thought and thought about what it should feel like," she said. "And then when I rode I made it feel the same way."

*   *   *

CAROLE RETURNED TO her friends. "I'd say this day has been just about perfect," she said.

"It's entirely perfect," Lisa replied. "Look!"

Carole looked. Before the drill had started, Max had put white buckets reading DONATIONS TO CARL near the exits of the stands. Now, as people were leaving, almost every one of them dropped something into the buckets. Some of them also stopped to talk to Judy. More people had come to the drill than they expected —CARL was going to make a lot of money!

"It's super." Just as Carole was saying that, someone hugged her hard from behind. "Hi, Dad," she said. "What did you think?"

"I think," said her father, "that for once Stevie was absolutely right. I am proud of you!"

13

LISA SLID INTO their favorite booth at TD's, an ice cream parlor not far from Pine Hollow. "Whew! When I think about all the work we've done today, I know I need some ice cream!"

"Ice cream and a Saddle Club meeting," said Stevie.

Carole only nodded. For the moment she felt too tired to speak. After the excitement of the drill, they'd had the work of cooling out the horses, untacking them, loading them and all their gear onto the horse trailer, and then, back at Pine Hollow, unloading them and settling them for the night.

"When I think of all the work we have waiting for

us tomorrow—" she began. All of her tack was filthy, and would have to be cleaned and oiled. Starlight would need a good grooming, her boots needed polishing—

"Don't," said Stevie.

"Don't what?"

"Don't think. At least not about tomorrow. Whatever we have to do then we'll still have to do whether we think about it or not. For now I think we should enjoy today."

"Here, here," Lisa said weakly. Maybe a double sundae would revive her.

The waitress came to take their order. It was the same waitress they had had many times before, and she frowned when she saw them. "You again," she said by way of greeting.

"Us again," Carole agreed. "And we're tired. I need something invigorating—I'll take a banana split."

Lisa raised an eyebrow, considering. Bananas? No. "I'll have a large turtle sundae with extra whipped cream," she decided.

The waitress swiveled to face Stevie, her face set. Lisa and Carole smiled. This was always fun.

"I think I'd like a sundae to commemorate my horse," Stevie said. "She was awfully good today.

She's a light-colored bay, almost chestnut. Do you have any chestnuts?"

"Absolutely not," the waitress said.

"What's the closest thing you have?"

"We've got chopped peanuts, whole peanuts, almond slivers, cashews, pecans, and walnuts in sauce."

"I'll take all of those," Stevie said. "And caramel sauce, since that's almost chestnut colored, and marshmallow sauce, since that sort of starts out the same as 'mare.' Let's see—all that on, make it fresh peach ice cream."

Carole choked. The waitress looked grim.

"And don't forget the cherry," Stevie said.

"I never do." The waitress stalked away.

"That was mean," Lisa said. "How could you order something like that?"

"I always eat it, don't I?" Stevie asked. "Besides, I don't think she really minds—I add color to her life."

"I'm not talking about the waitress," Lisa replied. "I'm talking about Belle. How could you commemorate her great performance by ordering a sundae that's completely nuts?"

Carole burst into laughter. Stevie looked appalled. "I didn't think of it that way." She thought hard. "We just won't tell Belle about it, okay? I wouldn't want her to get the wrong idea."

"Horses don't understand English, Stevie Lake," Carole intoned. It was something that Max said to them often.

"I just don't want to take any chances," Stevie replied.

Their sundaes arrived and they dug in happily. "I'm beginning to feel better," Carole announced. "Actually, I've been feeling fine, but I'm beginning to feel awake. I have to say, I didn't think things could possibly go so well today."

"Perfect," said Stevie. "They were perfect."

"They really were," Carole replied, "and I didn't think they would be. I really didn't think our crazy scheme would work."

Stevie looked offended. "My crazy schemes always work—at least, most of the time."

"The best part," Lisa said, "was getting Veronica to actually buy Jessica her dog. I never even *imagined* that."

"All I told Jessica was to come see me at the CARL booth," said Stevie. "I figured I could find some way to talk her mother into adopting a pet for her. But when I saw Veronica at exactly the right time—"

"Perfect," Carole said with satisfaction. "I would have been very happy if Veronica had made a donation to CARL, the way we planned. I'm thrilled that she made her donation to Jessica instead. But can you believe she had that much money? Twenty-eight dollars, plus what she gave us for fortunes!"

"In this case, I'm glad of it," said Lisa. "Jessica can use the rest to buy something for Buddy. I saw them getting into their car right before we left the fairgrounds. Do you know what Jessica said to me? She came running over, all breathless, and she said, 'You were right, Lisa! I do have a new best friend!'" Lisa grinned. "That really made me feel good."

"I'm so glad we could do something to help her," Carole said. "That alone was worth all of our work."

"Any one part of it was worth all of our work, in my opinion," Stevie said. "Just seeing Veronica diAngelo walk around in designer jeans she destroyed herself made it completely worthwhile to me." Stevie finished the rest of her sundae. "The Veronica/Michael triumph. What a wonderful day."

They sat in quiet satisfaction for a moment, but suddenly Lisa looked sad. "It's not a perfect day though," she told her friends. "I saw Judy Barker after the drill too. She told me that Doc Tock had stopped by the van. Sal, the horse at CARL, died this morning. They did everything they could to save him, but he was just too sick." Lisa sighed. She knew the memory of poor, neglected Sal was one she would never forget.

Carole patted her arm sympathetically. "It's worse for you because you met Sal," she said, "but I feel awful when a horse dies too."

"We all do," said Stevie. "Especially when it's for such a stupid reason. But, Lisa, you said all along that Sal might die. And all of us know that CARL can't do everything."

"But they can help," Lisa said. "I know that, and I know it's important. I'm really glad we worked so hard for CARL today too. When we help them, it's like we're helping animals like Sal."

"Today we did the best we could," Carole said. "At least we know that."

"This," said Lisa, "was one of the best Saddle Club projects of all."

They sat contented for a few minutes. "You know," Stevie was saying, "I could almost eat another sundae," when Lisa sat up and pointed out the window.

"Look at that!"

Stevie and Carole looked. Across the shopping mall, Michael Grant was walking into the audio store, Sights 'n' Sounds. He had his hands stuck in his pockets and he looked annoyed.

Veronica was following right on his heels. She was

wearing the same torn jeans and shirt she had on before, but now she'd added a scuzzy pair of plastic shower sandals to her ensemble.

"She looks *awful!*" Carole said.

"That's something to celebrate," commented Lisa.

Stevie raised her water glass. "Here's to the *new* Veronica!"

ABOUT THE AUTHOR

BONNIE BRYANT is the author of many books for young readers, including novelizations of movie hits such as *Teenage Mutant Ninja Turtles*® and *Honey, I Blew Up the Kid*, written under her married name, B. B. Hiller.

Ms. Bryant began writing The Saddle Club in 1986. Although she had done some riding before that, she intensified her studies then and found herself learning right along with her characters Stevie, Carole, and Lisa. She claims that they are all much better riders than she is.

Ms. Bryant was born and raised in New York City. She still lives there, in Greenwich Village, with her two sons.

DON'T MISS BONNIE BRYANT'S NEXT EXCITING
SADDLE CLUB ADVENTURE . . .

STABLE GROOM
THE SADDLE CLUB #45

Stevie, Carole, and Lisa are ecstatic that stable owner Max
Regnery III is about to marry. They can't resist being part
of things, so they plan a surprise "bridle" shower for the
groom-to-be.

Some serious business also needs their attention. The
girls want stablehand Red to become a certified riding
counselor. Maybe that way, he can be in charge of Pine
Hollow Stables while Max is honeymooning and he'll get
some respect from bossy Veronica diAngelo.

It looks as if disaster will strike when both plans are
marred by a mix-up that only The Saddle Club could
cause!

THE SADDLE CLUB ™

❑ 15594-6 HORSE CRAZY #1	$3.50/$4.50 Can.	
❑ 15611-X HORSE SHY #2	$3.25/$3.99 Can.	
❑ 15626-8 HORSE SENSE #3	$3.50/$4.50 Can.	
❑ 15637-3 HORSE POWER #4	$3.50/$4.50 Can.	
❑ 15703-5 TRAIL MATES #5	$3.50/$4.50 Can.	
❑ 15728-0 DUDE RANCH #6	$3.50/$4.50 Can.	
❑ 15754-X HORSE PLAY #7	$3.25/$3.99 Can.	
❑ 15769-8 HORSE SHOW #8	$3.25/$3.99 Can.	
❑ 15780-9 HOOF BEAT #9	$3.50/$4.50 Can.	
❑ 15790-6 RIDING CAMP #10	$3.50/$4.50 Can.	
❑ 15805-8 HORSE WISE #11	$3.25/$3.99 Can..	
❑ 15821-X RODEO RIDER #12	$3.50/$4.50 Can.	
❑ 15832-5 STARLIGHT CHRISTMAS #13	$3.50/$4.50 Can.	
❑ 15847-3 SEA HORSE #14	$3.50/$4.50 Can.	
❑ 15862-7 TEAM PLAY #15	$3.50/$4.50 Can.	
❑ 15882-1 HORSE GAMES #16	$3.25/$3.99 Can.	
❑ 15937-2 HORSENAPPED #17	$3.50/$4.50 Can.	
❑ 15928-3 PACK TRIP #18	$3.50/$4.50 Can.	

❑ 15938-0 STAR RIDER #19	$3.50/$4.50 Can.
❑ 15907-0 SNOW RIDE #20	$3.50/$4.50 Can.
❑ 15983-6 RACEHORSE #21	$3.50/$4.50 Can.
❑ 15990-9 FOX HUNT #22	$3.50/$4.50 Can.
❑ 48025-1 HORSE TROUBLE #23	$3.50/$4.50 Can.
❑ 48067-7 GHOST RIDER #24	$3.50/$4.50 Can.
❑ 48072-3 SHOW HORSE #25	$3.50/$4.50 Can.
❑ 48073-1 BEACH RIDE #26	$3.50/$4.50 Can.
❑ 48074-X BRIDLE PATH #27	$3.50/$4.50 Can.
❑ 48075-8 STABLE MANNERS #28	$3.50/$4.50 Can.
❑ 48076-6 RANCH HANDS #29	$3.50/$4.50 Can.
❑ 48077-4 AUTUMN TRAIL #30	$3.50/$4.50 Can.
❑ 48145-2 HAYRIDE #31	$3.50/$4.50 Can.
❑ 48146-0 CHOCOLATE HORSE #32	$3.50/$4.50 Can.
❑ 48147-9 HIGH HORSE #33	$3.50/$4.50 Can.
❑ 48148-7 HAY FEVER #34	$3.50/$4.50 Can.
❑ 48149-5 A SUMMER WITHOUT HORSES Super #1	$3.99/$4.99 Can.

Bantam Doubleday Dell
Books For Young Readers

Bantam Books, Dept. SC35,
2451 South Wolf Road,Des Plaines, IL 60018   DA60

Please send the items I have checked above. I am enclosing $_____ (please add $2.50 to cover postage and handling). Send check or money order, no cash or C.O.D.s please.

Mr/Ms _____

Address _____

City/State _____   Zip _____

Please allow four to six weeks for delivery.
Prices and availability subject to change without notice.   SC35-4/94